THE TROUBLE BEGINS

linda himelblau

DELACORTE PRESS

Published by
Delacorte Press
an imprint of
Random House Children's Books
a division of Random House, Inc.
New York

Text copyright © 2005 by Linda Himelblau
Jacket illustration copyright © 2005 by Tom Nick Cocotos

Visit us on the Web! www.randomhouse.com/kids
Educators and librarians, for a variety of teaching tools, visit us
at www.randomhouse.com/teachers

Library of Congress Cataloging-in-Publication Data

Himelblau, Linda.
The trouble begins / Linda Himelblau.
p. cm.
Summary: Reunited with his family for the first time since he was a baby, fifth grader Du struggles to adapt to his new home in the United States.
ISBN 0-385-73273-2 (trade : alk. paper) — ISBN 0-385-90288-3 (glb : alk. paper) [1. Vietnamese Americans—Fiction. 2. Immigrants—Fiction. 3. Family—Fiction. 4. Vietnam—Emigration and immigration—Fiction. 5. Schools—Fiction.] I. Title.
PZ7.H5679Tr 2005
[Fic]—dc 22
2004028253

The text of this book is set in 12-point Goudy.

Book design by Kenny Holcomb

Printed in the United States of America

November 2005

10 9 8 7 6 5 4 3 2 1

BVG

To Irv

A New Home

A bunch of people I don't know pat me on the head, which I hate, and tell me what a lucky boy I am and how happy I must be. I don't feel lucky and I'm not happy. I am shaking even though the sun is shining but when they pull a scratchy blanket over me I push it off because I am suddenly as hot as a lizard lying in the sun. I wish I was a lizard. I could lie down on the ground and not move for hours and sleep and sleep and not talk and I would run if anyone tried to pat me on the head.

My mother is in a hurry to go. "I need to get home before

dark," she tells the people. "We must hurry. Good-bye. Good-bye." I wonder what bad thing will happen in the dark. A few minutes ago I saw my mother for the first time since I was a little baby so I stare and stare at her but she just looks like a regular woman to me. Maybe it is because my eyes are blurry and want to close and my ears are ringing so all the talking is blurred too. In the crowd of people that shouted at us in the airport she was the one who leaned down to me and whispered, "I am your mother, Du," so I could barely hear her. She stared at me too until a man who said he is my uncle pushed me toward the car. The American air outside smelled like gasoline. Five lines of cars crept by, starting and stopping, and the car they put me into blocked one of the rows. Car horns honked.

I see how carefully the woman who is my mother helps my grandma into the backseat next to me. We came together on the plane and my mother has not seen my grandma for all those years either. My grandma is sick but she has been sick for a long time. I am sick from riding on the airplane while days and nights went by outside the little window. Being in America will make my grandma better, everyone says. When she was sick I took care of her. I don't tell them I'm sick in case she needs me to take care of her here.

"Hurry," pleads my mother to the girl who says she is my sister. Thuy or Lin? I don't know which one and no one tells me. She is hugging everyone and saying good-bye too many times. I don't know her either. When she gets in the front seat next to my mother I know she talks too loud. She shouts back at my grandma about food she cooked for her and a room she fixed for her but all my grandma wants to do is sleep. Me too. My loud sister can't see this.

The faces of the uncles and aunts and cousins come close to the window. "Good-bye, good-bye," they yell through the glass. I make sure my grandma is okay. I fold up my jacket to make a pillow for her. Her eyes are closed. As the car jerks away my stomach feels funny and I hear a high pinging noise in my ears that won't stop. I want to see America but when I look out the window my head sways and my stomach is tight like it's tied in a knot. I close my eyes.

"Fasten your seat belt," orders my loud sister. I keep my eyes closed. "You better do what I say, Du!" she says. "You don't know how dangerous it is not to fasten your seat belt." Days ago, on the way to the airport in the Philippines, my grandma and I rode in the back of a rattly truck crowded with people and bags and boxes. The bumpy road made us fly off our seats. I got in fast to get a good place for my grandma near the front but then I had to hang on sitting on the edge of the tailgate. Nobody had a seat belt. I don't do anything.

"Please, Du," says the woman who is my mother. "I am not used to driving a car and especially driving on the freeway. Please fasten Grandmother's too." The seat belts are like on the airplane. I dig behind the seat to find them and fasten my grandma's carefully so I don't wake her up. I don't fasten mine. I'm not scared.

My mother leans forward as she drives. I can see that the

knuckles of her hands are white where she holds on to the steering wheel like we would fly away if she let go. She jerks the car one way and then another. My sister grabs a little handle above the door with one hand. Her knuckles are white too. She talks in a shrill excited voice. "Get in the right lane. Put on your turn signal. We have to get on here. We have to go south. Look out, look out." Other cars swerve fast around us. One of the drivers honks. My blurry eyes close. I think that I will learn how to drive. I will drive fast and swerve around all the slow people. I will drive my mother wherever she wants to go.

• • •

I wake up sometimes but we are always in the lines of cars, either going fast or suddenly slowing so we don't move at all. Finally I wake up to my sister calling out, "Wake up! Wake up! We're almost home." I open my eyes. I am hot and hair is plastered to my forehead, wet with sweat. Behind my eyes there is a steady pounding like a deep drum. I have dreamed of this coming-home moment ever since my grandma told me the tickets had come. I stare out the window. I don't see the tall sky-touching buildings of America. I see a skinny street with cars parked on both sides. I see little houses shaped like boxes, each with a fence around it. Inside their fences the doors of the houses are closed and the windows are covered, shutting out the air and the sun. Some have metal bars across the windows too. Sometimes there is a house where the front is green with grass and bright with

4

flowers but most of them are weedy and brown waiting for the rain. The car jerks to a stop. The knot in my stomach tightens. The front of the car is in a little space but my mother, jerking the car back and forth, can't get the back in. The house where she stops is one with green grass and flowers and a tall shady tree in front. I touch my grandma's hand. We are home.

The door on my grandma's side of the car is pulled open. A short angry-looking man is there. He bows to my grandma with both hands pressed together at his chest. It is my father, my grandma's son. I see that the angriness in his face hides tears. I know and my sister knows that it is not our time to speak. My father helps my grandma out. She is so tiny he almost lifts her off her feet. I am dizzy and my head pounds. I push open the door on my side and step out into the street. My sister screams. There is a screech of brakes and a truck horn blares. Where I stand in the street I look into the angry red face of the American truck driver. He bangs the side of his truck with his hand. He yells at me but I only understand a little English from my Philippine school. It was more fun to play marbles than it was to listen to English. English puts me to sleep. With little screeches of the tires the driver lurches his truck around me and drives off. Now four people yell at me in Vietnamese.

"Watch out! You'll get killed doing that."

"Du, you've got to be careful here."

"Why'd you do that? This is a busy street!"

"Get out of that street!"

My mother and my grandma look at me too but they

don't yell. I look back at the family that I have only seen in a few pictures. The sister from the front seat who looks older than the other and must be Thuy. Another sister with glasses and her arms wrapped around a fat book she holds to her chest, who is Lin. A big brother who looks like he eats too much, who is Vuong. A father who holds out a hand to me while he supports my grandmother with his other hand. I walk over. I shake his hand. We learned at school that this is what you do in America. My head whirls like I am turning fast in a circle. I don't want them to know I am sick. They talk in Vietnamese but even then I can't understand because of the dizziness.

A big white truck with writing on it pulls up behind the car. Again a horn honks. My father carefully gives my grandma to my mother and sister to support. He is my father; I try to believe this through the blur, watching him, seeing how he loves my grandma too. Happiness mixes with my dizziness and fever. Then, as he turns from my grandma, he changes. His face turns grim and hard. He yells in English to the truck driver, jumps two steps at a time to the porch, but not the porch of the bright house with the green grass and the tree and the flowers. He runs up the broken steps of the house next to it where the paint is peeling, and dusty brown weeds fill the front yard. He grabs an old suitcase and runs to the street. The truck screeches off almost before he closes its door behind him with the heavy suitcase balanced on his lap. My happiness disappears. All those years he left us in the Philippines and now he leaves again after a few minutes. Sometimes I thought my grandma stayed alive just

6

to see him. I am scared for a second. I took care of her in the Philippines but I don't know if I can do that in America without knowing English, without money or a car. Me, who never was scared in the Philippines. I would do anything to get stuff my grandma needed. Now I just want to lie down. We turn again to go into the house. I wish I could just lie down outside on the stairs.

"Lady!" Now another angry voice shouts in English. A stream of bossy-sounding words follows. A tall old man leaning over the wire fence between the beautiful green yard and the one that is my father's is yelling at my mother and pointing at the car.

My mother beckons for my big brother to support my grandma. "Sorry, sorry," she whispers, bowing to the tall old white man. She hurries to move the car. In spite of my blurry eyes and my whirling head I give the old man a mean look. I follow the others into the house. My sister is excited. She shows my grandma a little room with bright curtains and a bed where she can lie down. I lie down on the floor in the corner. They tell me I can't sleep there but I cover my head with my jacket and I don't listen to them and I try to stop the whirling in my brain.

● ● ●

I sleep for a long time. When I wake up someone has moved me to my brother's room to sleep on one side of his bed. I sleep some more and sometimes the window is light when I wake up and sometimes it is dark. Now I pretend to sleep so I won't have to eat the terrible food they bring to me. My sister, the one called Thuy, brings noodles in salty yellow-colored water with little tiny squares of chicken floating in it. The noodles are so small and squishy they look like pond scum. The other sister, Lin, brings a green drink in a plastic bottle. I drink it so fast I throw up.

"He can't sleep in my room anymore! He smells and he's a bad-luck kid," whispers my brother, Vuong, who thinks I am asleep.

"Give him a chance," Thuy answers. "He just got here."

"That's what I mean," argues Vuong. "He just got here. He's had English lessons for years over there but he's so stupid he doesn't know how to speak it. He got Grandma sick so she's in the hospital and now he got Dad so sick he can hardly walk. What if he can't go to work and Mr. Vronsky fires him? All he cares about is money. He'll be hard on all of us."

"That's not true," Thuy answers so softly I can hardly hear her.

"Well, even if the kid doesn't get Dad fired, he's throwing up in *my* room. He's a bad-luck kid. He can sleep on the couch." Vuong pushes me with his toe. "Wake up, Du," he says. He holds his nose away from me and gives me a rag to wipe up the floor. He leads me down the hall to the room with the couch and the TV. For the first time in my life I will sleep in a room all by myself. "Don't you throw up on that couch," he warns me as he leaves.

Bluuh! Cough, cough! Bluuh! I make sounds just like throwing up.

Vuong whirls around. He sees that I fooled him. He stomps out. I go back to sleep worrying about my grandma. We couldn't come to America for all those years because we had something called TB. Now we are cured of that but she has gotten this new sickness from me. I want to see her more than I want anything. More than I want to be back in the Philippines. But she is in the hospital and I can't go. Vuong says our dad cares most about money. It cost a lot to bring us here and hospitals cost a lot too. I wonder if I can pay him back.

I wake up later still hot and dizzy and not knowing where I am but I am aware somebody is looking at me. I keep my eyes squeezed shut until I hear him cough. I open my eyes the tiniest slit and I can see my dad standing there looking down at me. I squeeze them shut again because I don't know what to say. He knows, though; he knows I am awake. "You go to school," he says in his voice that is hoarse like mine from the sickness. "You go to school. You work hard. You'll be all right." I hear him turn and shuffle away to bed but there is still nothing I can think of to say. I'll be the best at school, I think.

● ● ●

After a few more days I get better. I eat the food because I am so hungry. Most of it comes from cans because my grandma is still in the hospital and my mother is at the hospital staying with her or at work or sleeping. When she sees me in the early morning, she smiles kindly at me and asks me if I want food. She sees that I love peaches and cherries so she brings them especially for me. Vuong complains. My father is usually angry when I see him. His face is grim and furrowed and he slams doors and walks with heavy feet. I think he blames me for getting my grandma sick and for getting him sick and for costing extra money. I stay away from him. Later he will see how smart I am and how I can make money too. Ever since I was little my grandma has called me a dragon. Everyone knows dragons are smart and lucky.

When I go in the dining room I can see that tall old white man spying on us through the window from his house next door. I sit on the floor and look from behind the pot on the window ledge. He doesn't know I can see his wrinkly old hand pulling back the curtain. He's an American with a big nose and bushy eyebrows. He should take those eyebrows and grow them on top of his head where he doesn't have any hair at all. If he wants to watch something why doesn't he watch TV?

Nothing interesting ever happens here. My sisters and my brother sit there studying from big fat books even though it's summer vacation now. That old man won't see me sitting there studying because I won't do it even when they boss me. I decide to give him something exciting to watch. I get a big knife out of the kitchen and sneak up behind my big sister, Thuy, like I'm going to murder her while she's reading. I walk very softly in my bare feet. I raise the knife high over my head so the old man's sure to see it.

"Du, you get out of here right now! I'm trying to study. Go someplace else and fool around," Thuy shouts. She's mad because I made her look up from her big fat book. I check the window. She jumps up from her chair and chases me back into the kitchen.

"Don't run with a knife," shouts my other sister, Lin. That old man still doesn't call 911. Vuong told me that's the number to call if something bad happens. The old man doesn't call even if somebody might get murdered. I'm getting mad at him watching us all the time like we're some sort of TV show. He's been watching since the first day my grandma and me came when he yelled at my mom about the car. I saw him spying outside then, hanging over his fence. I'm gonna figure out a way to fix him. I go sit on the window ledge with my back to the old man's window and I bounce Thuy's big eraser from one of my feet to the other. Once I get up to eighteen times in a row.

● ● ●

"Du, stop that!" Thuy yells.

"What?" I yell back, because I'm not doing anything.

"Smacking on a banana and kicking the wall," says Lin with a sniff. She's a year younger than Thuy but just as bossy. I fall off the window ledge and stomp around the table. Vuong swats backward at me with his hand. I'm quick. I stick out the bottom part of the banana. His hand mashes against it. He jumps up. I run. This is fun. He's so slow he can never catch me. He chases me out the front door. I wait until he almost grabs me. Then I take the fast way down. I vault over the railing on the front porch. *Crack!* The no-good railing breaks. I crash to the ground with pieces of the railing all around me. I jump up to laugh at him so he knows it didn't hurt and he still can't catch me.

"Now you've done it!" he shouts as he slams the door. I hear him turn the lock. I try to put the railing back but some of the posts broke right off. I can see little holes in the wood. I crouch down where there's sun to see better. Little bugs made the holes. I blow in them. Wood dust comes out. I stick a little stick in the hole to see if a bug will come out.

"Your dad's gonna have to fix that." It's that old spy from next door yelling from across his fence. He's been watching me the whole time. I don't even look up. "You better get some shoes with all those splinters around." I'm not sure of all the words he says but I know what he really means. He hopes I get splinters in all my toes. I still don't look up. Americans wear shoes too much. They wear them in their own houses. My mom says it's dirty. I wonder if that old man wears shoes when he goes to bed. I prop the railing against the broken posts on the porch.

Our street is empty except for some little kids behind a fence in a front yard. In the Philippines there were kids everywhere but in America the kids are all hiding. When I hear the roar of an engine I trot down the street. I've seen a guy who fixes his truck in his front yard. My sister says he's from Mexico and I should leave him alone but I don't think it will hurt anything if I just watch. Today he's straining and groaning to pull something out from under the hood of his truck. He doesn't even see me. Sweat runs down his face to his bushy black mustache. I go close enough to see what he's pulling on. It's a big round heavy thing deep in the engine. His hands are black with grease. *Crack!* "Oof!" He falls backward; the part he was pulling on comes loose and crashes down on the fender. He whacks into me because I'm trying to see from behind him.

"*¡Cuidado!*" he yells. It's Mexican so I don't know what it means but he looks angry, like what happened is my fault. I run away around the truck. He heaves the round thing on the ground and shakes his hand because he scraped it pulling out the heavy engine part. He doesn't come after me so I lean over the front end to see what's inside. "Hold this," he says in English. He tosses me a plastic piece with three wires hanging out. I hold it until he reaches out his hand. We both lean into the truck engine to see. I help him hold the wires in place while he connects them. I wish he would tell me what everything is called. I know some of the words in Vietnamese. When it's too dark he wipes off his hands. "*Gracias,*" he says with a nod. I know it's Mexican so I say, "*Chao tam biet,*" good-bye in Vietnamese. I go home.

Vuong doesn't tell my dad how the railing broke. My dad's too busy to worry about an old railing because he and my mom have to hurry to visit my grandma in the hospital.

● ● ●

I just watch TV for days and days. My mom and dad go to work, then to the hospital, then to sleep. I can't go to the hospital with them because I'm too young. When they're home sometimes I see them staring at me. I stare at them too

13

when they aren't looking. I say to myself, "That's my mom and dad," so it will seem real. When he has a little time my dad teaches me American stuff like red-light crossing and shopping in stores with aisles so long I get lost once. My mom buys me American clothes, just like the Philippine clothes only brand-new. The shoes feel like heavy weights on my legs. But mostly my mom and dad are busy. Thuy and Lin and Vuong go someplace every day too. Summer school, they say. I am glad because when they are home they try to boss me around.

"You should practice reading, Du."

"You should wear socks, Du."

"Do you know your multiplication tables, Du? You should practice."

"You should comb your hair, Du."

"What's this called in English, Du? Do you know?"

"Talk English, Du."

I just watch TV and don't listen to them after a while. I look for pictures on TV that look like the Philippines. When I see kids outside and go to mess around with them they look at me funny and ride away on their bikes. In the Philippines kids would be excited and yell, "Here comes Du." We all messed around together even if we didn't know each other. Here there are mostly just cars outside.

The Trouble Begins

On the first day I know I don't like American school. When I get a chance I'm going to leave. I don't like the teacher because I don't know what she's saying. She points at me and motions for me to stand up. Then she says a lot of words and one of them is *Du*. Everyone laughs. She smiles a big fake smile. She points for me to sit next to a Mexican girl who eats too much. "This is Veronica," the teacher says. "She'll help you. Can you say, 'Hello, Veronica'?"

I think I know what she wants but I don't want help from this girl. I don't say anything. The teacher repeats what she said and kids are starting to giggle. Finally I mutter, "Hello, Veronica," so she'll quit asking and Veronica reaches out and grabs my hand with her sweaty one and says, "Hello, Du." Everyone laughs again. I'm not saying stuff like that ever again. Veronica whispers to me about what stuff to put in my desk and where to write my name on papers until the teacher gives her a mean look. I wasn't going to do it her way anyway.

There are lots of other things I don't like about school the first day. I don't like how the tag on my new T-shirt scratches my neck, so I rip it out. "Ohhh, you made a hole," whispers Veronica. I stuff the tag into her pencil case. I don't like how the teacher talks and talks and then writes "Assignment: Four beautiful paragraphs about your summer vacation" on the blackboard. Underneath she writes what kids tell her they did.

"We went to Disneyland twice in one week," says a girl in pink shoes.

"We camped out for three days at Yosemite." I know Disneyland but I don't know Yosemite. I quit listening. The teacher writes other places: grandparents' house, Girl Scout camp, Sea World. Everyone starts writing but me. I don't know how to write English. I know what *vacation* is but I never had one.

"Please try, Du," the teacher says as she walks by and taps her finger on my blank paper. I still can't write English no matter how many times she says please even though earlier she said it was a magic word.

I don't like it when a lady comes to take me away from

the class. "Come with me, Du," she says, smiling. "This will be fun. I'm going to test your reading." It isn't fun. We sit in a little room with books and papers piled everywhere. She gives me a paper with hundreds of little words, close together, and says, "Just start here." I can't read the words. "That's fine, Du," she says after a while even though I didn't read anything. "Now try this." She gives me a paper with fewer words in bigger letters. I glance at it and shrug and look away. At the end she gives me a paper with just a few big words on it. I know some of the words but I don't read because then she'd know I couldn't read the others. She shakes her head and writes on her papers. She leads me to the door. "You know the way back to class, don't you, Du?" she asks. I nod because I know the way but after she closes the door I sneak between the office building and the first bunch of classrooms. I climb over the high wire fence before anyone sees me. I don't need to go to school, I think. I'll save my parents' money and I'll go to school later when I can learn important stuff instead of what I did on my summer vacation.

I walk by the market store on the way home. The first time I went to the store with Thuy I couldn't believe how big it was or how much food was there. The aisles were as long as streets and food was stacked from our feet to above our heads in every direction. I asked her about some black kids hanging around by the door. "They make money helping people carry out their groceries," she said. "Don't look at them. We don't need any help." I saw one push a lady's cart to her car.

17

"I can do that," I said.

"No, you can't," Thuy exploded. "Stay away from here. They won't like it if you take their job." Now when I walk by I see that the black kids who worked there are all gone. They must be in school too. I'll help people and make money, I think. It'll be better than going to school. I run up to people coming out the door and say, "Help, lady, help." Most of them shake their heads or say, "No thanks," but finally one lets me push her cart. She gives me two quarters. I learn fast which people will want help. One lady gives me a dollar. When I see the black kids coming after school I go home with my pocket full of money.

From down the street I see people on our front porch: white people, Thuy and Lin and Vuong, a man in a brown uniform, and my dad. I know by now it's never good when my dad has to leave work during the day so I reach into my pocket to hold the money I made. He will be happy to see that, to see how easily I can make money here. I jog down the street and they all turn to look when Thuy points at me. That old white man from next door is leaning over the fence looking too. Everyone talks at once, English and Vietnamese, when I walk up the porch stairs. Angry voices tell me how I shouldn't do this and that and how much trouble I cause. I know Vietnamese kids wait to talk until the adults are finished but everybody on the porch sounds like they'll talk forever.

"I'm making money," I announce loudly over the talking. "Vuong can teach me school stuff at home and I'll make money." I hold out my hand with all the coins in it. There's

18

a sudden silence. Then the last thing I ever expect happens. My dad slaps my hand and the coins clatter all over the porch.

"You go to school!" he shouts back at me. He turns, stomps down the stairs and screeches away in his car. The school people talk and talk to me and my mom, who probably doesn't know what they are saying much more than I do. When they leave I go to the back of our house. I leave the money scattered all over the porch.

I'm tired of hearing talking and I don't know what my dad wants. He says he wants money but then he wants school. Does he know the dumb stuff they do at American school? Later I sneak in but Thuy and Lin and Vuong hear me.

"What are you doing to Ba and Ma?" growls Thuy in English but she gets mixed up and uses Ba and Ma for Dad and Mom. Then she switches to Vietnamese even though she said before she would only talk to me in English so I'd learn. "You're a stupid," she whispers. "Why do you think you can just run away from school?"

"You make it so hard for Ba!" Lin butts in. "He hates fixing toilets and working for Mr. Vronsky and if he has to keep leaving work because of you he can even lose that job. Then we won't have any money."

"I got money," I argue.

"He owned land in Vietnam and he rented his land to farmers and now you come here and pull him down to the bottom again," whispers Vuong. I can tell he's proud that Ba had land in Vietnam.

"In America school is free but you have to go or they put your parents in jail," adds Thuy.

"No, they don't," I scoff.

"They do too," all three of them snap at once.

"They could have brought Ma's sister and her mother but they saved and saved and brought you and you're just a bad-luck kid," Vuong says.

They keep repeating themselves in that bossy, hissing whisper. Suddenly I understand. They are whispering because Grandma is home. I run out of the kitchen and into her room and there she is. She opens her eyes and she sees me and reaches out her hand and smiles. I take her hand, like a little bird claw, and I hold it. I'll ask her about all this stuff later, I think. Everything is okay if she is alive and she is here.

● ● ●

That night on the couch I remember the night my dad stood over me while I pretended to sleep. "You go to school. You work hard," he said. I worked hard today because I thought he wanted money the most. Now I know he wants me to go to school. Even if they just do stupid things there. What the others said is true. In America school is free but you have to go. He thinks I brought bad luck with me but when I see my family I don't think they were so lucky before I came either. My grandma says I'm a dragon and dragons are the luckiest.

● ● ●

I go to school now every day even though I hate it. I'm still not talking there. Except I talk just a little so they won't know that I'm not talking. They'll just think I'm stupid and don't know any answers. They think I'm stupid anyway. We read a story about a "dear little mouse" that saves food for the winter. In the Philippines I squashed the "dear little mice" so they wouldn't ruin the food and my grandma and I would have enough to eat. Veronica, who's really stupid, always tells me when it's time to go to my superdumb reading group in Room 10.

"You better go, Du," she whispers even though my teacher, whose name is Mrs. Dorfman, has forgotten. If I'm quiet she'll forget all about me.

"You better go doo-doo, Du Du," whispers Jorge. When I jump up to hit him Mrs. Dorfman remembers.

"Time for reading, Du," she says. She's glad when I leave.

Everybody in Room 10 is really dumb except me and I'm not talking. I'll read when I have to but I won't talk. Thuy and Lin and Vuong talk just like Americans and sometimes they talk so fast I can't understand them and neither can my mom and dad. My sisters say they think in English but I don't believe them. It's too hard. Everybody talks Vietnamese to my grandma. If they heard that at school they'd really laugh. At recess Anthony pushes up the corners of his eyes and goes, "Ching ching chong dong." It's supposed to be Vietnamese but he's so stupid he doesn't even know what it sounds like. But everybody laughs. Then I grab his dumb baseball hat and throw it on the roof. The playground aide sees and I get sent to the Counseling Center. I write "I will respect the rights and property of others" one hundred times. Then I go back to the class and crunch Anthony's pencil when it rolls under my desk.

Mrs. Dorfman smiles at the end of the day. "Don't forget, students. Jamestown dioramas are due tomorrow. Check your homework assignment sheets so you have all the components." I hear her say *due* so I listen but it's not about me.

I walk with some guys from my class on the way home but they don't talk to me. They laugh a lot and I make sure they're not laughing at me by giving them mean looks whenever they start. If I hear *Du* or *Du Du* they're going to be sorry. Before my street they all turn and go a different way. I go down the alley behind the houses because it's more interesting.

"Free Cooper Farms Chicken!" say the big red letters on the newspaper. I can read *free* and *farm* and *chicken* easily because they're in even bigger letters than the ones in my dumb reading book. Lots of stuff in America is free. I pick up the newspaper near the trash can and shake off the dirt. I tear off the "Free Chicken" part. I'll take home a feast for everybody, free. I open some trash cans even though they're smelly, and I find another "Free Chicken" paper. By the time I get all the way down the alley I have six free chickens. I know the free chickens are at the big market on Fortieth Street because I see the name when we shop. I jog over there to get my chickens.

Inside I pick six of the biggest chickens to put in my basket. When I wait in line there's a kid from school behind me. I know him even though he's in another class because he doesn't play softball or Three Flies Up at recess. He stands around like me. He doesn't say hi so I don't either. He's with his dad, who's way too tall and skinny and has a big hairy beard that's so ugly I can't look at it. It looks dirty. They talk and talk to each other while we wait and sometimes they laugh but I can't understand what they're saying. My dad never talks to me like that, like he's just a kid himself, and he never talks to Thuy or Lin or Vuong either. He works too hard to just mess around chattering like a kid.

My turn finally comes. I heave my six chickens onto the counter. The lady drags them across the scanner. "That'll be forty-eight dollars and seventy-two cents," she says. I hand her the "Free Chicken" papers.

"What's this?" she demands.

"Free chicken," I answer loudly so she knows I can read it.

She pounds on a little bell on her counter. People turn and stare. A man in a brown jacket with the store name on it hurries over. The lady talks to him so everybody can hear.

"Where did you get these, young man?" He waves my "Free Chicken" papers in my face. I don't want to say that I got them out of trash cans so I shrug. He rips them in two. "Come with me," he commands. He keeps talking about taking things from mailboxes and calling the police. When we walk by the front door I run for it. I'm out the door and down the street before he can grab me or get anyone else to grab me. I hear him yelling behind me. I'm glad the kid from school didn't know me or he might tell the man my name. This country cheats. They say things are free when they're not.

When I get home I sneak in the back door but Thuy and Lin are in the kitchen. "Get some soda," they order me. "Clear off the table." I clear the dirty dishes and the teapot and the potato chips off the table. My grandma is still too sick to cook good food and my mom works late every day. I don't have any chickens for a chicken feast. We have to eat American frozen food with slimy cheese. Thuy and Lin and Vuong tear off big pieces of pizza even though Thuy didn't cook it long enough. I pull strings of cheese off mine. I eat little bites. "Du, do you have homework?" asks Thuy like she's my boss.

"Nope," I say, the way Anthony always says it at school with a tricky smile and my head tipped back.

"Then you do dishes," orders Thuy. I don't care. Pizza plates and soda glasses. When they're done I pour hot water over dried-up American noodles in a white foam cup. I slurp up the noodles and go see if my grandma wants some. She's asleep.

I watch the TV while American people laugh and laugh but I don't know what's funny. Nothing, I think. Channel eleven has a bear running around at night getting into people's garbage cans. Vuong comes in. "Gimme the remote," he orders. I sit on it. The channel changes. I bounce up and down on the remote and the channel changes again and again. We laugh.

"What's a Jamestown diorama?" I ask him.

Forty minutes later we have a shoe box with one side cut off. Inside there's a paper fort leaning over and some trees leaning further over and a river made of foil from the pizza that looks like pizza foil.

"There," says Vuong. "You've got a Jamestown diorama to turn in tomorrow."

"It's ugly," I say.

Vuong laughs. "You waited too long to start," he says. "Better ugly than not at all."

Vuong would never take anything that ugly to school. Thuy and Lin laugh when they see it. I wait until they go to bed. Like the bears I sneak out to the garbage cans. I push my Jamestown diorama deep down under the garbage bags. I'm not taking that ugly thing to school. Maybe I'll make a good one. The best one in the class.

● ● ●

I still see that old man from next door spying on our house through our window. If he spies on our house all day when I'm at school our fat Buddha with his big wide smile is going to be laughing back at him. The Buddha will sometimes give you things if you ask right but he wouldn't give anything to that old man. That old spy must wonder about the pictures of people from Vietnam and the red lights that look like candles. I wonder about the pictures too but when I ask, Thuy says, "Shut up, Du." When I ask Lin she says not to ask because they're all dead from the war and it makes Ba and Ma sad to talk about them and it might bring the evil from over there to here.

When I look in the old man's yard I can see great big fat juicy blackberries growing up his back wall. He's got a shed back there where he keeps his lawn mower and he's the only one on the alley who has a big cement block wall to keep everybody out. The cement blocks are like they had in the Philippines and I know they can't keep me out. I'm going to get some of those berries. That's the price he has to pay for looking in our window all the time. I could vault over the wire fence between our side yards in one second but he might see me from his spying window. I'll climb over the big alley wall. I'll eat berries and I'll even bring some home. If he sees me and yells I'll be over the wall before he can get his old man legs down the back steps.

● ● ●

I scraped my knee and my elbow but I got here. I hope Ma doesn't notice the hole in my new pants. Hey, cat! I'm not the only one up here. "Here, cat-cat. How did you get up here? Do you belong to that old man? I think you're wild like a tiger except you're gray like the wall. That old man can't catch either one of us. Watch!" I jump down into his yard so I don't wreck any of the berries climbing down.

These berries are good American food. I never saw any

like them before. In the Philippines we'd raid banana trees. I was the leader. We'd run in every direction if the farmer saw us so he didn't know which one to run after. We'd meet on the field behind the market road. We'd eat bananas and sometimes they were green and made us sick. But this old man's berries are sweet and juicy. They're so juicy I drip some on my shirt.

● ● ●

"Du, answer the door. We're studying," Thuy yells. No one comes to visit us except people selling stuff. I lift up the corner of the blanket I tacked over the living room window so I could see the TV better and sleep later in the morning. Now I see a police car in front and two policemen at the front door.

"Answer the door," Thuy yells when it rings again. I just sit in the corner of the couch. My heart is pumping hard. Why would police come to our house? Are they here about me? In the Philippines the police sprayed water cannons and tear gas on some men for getting together in the street at night. The police were afraid they'd riot to get more food. I saw a man get arrested here on Fortieth Street when I was coming home from school. He was handcuffed and pushed into the police car. My mind races around thinking about stuff I've done. I hope they don't take me away because I ran away from school or because I tried to get free chickens at the market or I picked some berries. There's a bowl of berries next to my grandma's bed. I put them there so she'd have something good when she woke up. I see little pimples of fear on my arm. Nobody arrested kids and grandmothers in the Philippines.

I pull back the blanket again and look sideways at the front door. The two policemen are talking to Thuy now. One of them's a lady. Thuy is using her nicest voice.

"He's our little brother," she says. "We're so sorry. He just came two months ago from overseas. The family was separated. He had a hard time. We'll tell him he can't just pick berries because he sees them. He didn't know. We're so sorry."

I did not have a hard time. I had a great time. Better than here. I had banana raids and swimming in the ocean and going to school only when my grandma could pay. I didn't have to sit with big fat books at the table and eat slimy cheese. I hear the police talk but their American is too fast to know what they say. I watch them walk down the stairs. I wasn't really scared and now I know it was that old man who tried to get me arrested. This means war.

I watch from the window while the spy slams out of his gate and stalks over to the policemen. He's waving his arms in the air and pointing at my house. They talk to him and the lady policeman puts a hand on his arm to calm him down. He's still sputtering after them when they get in their black and white car and drive away. That old man called the police because I took a few of his berries. I'm going to call the police next time he looks in our window. Thuy marches back to her studying but she yells, "Du, you stupid!" when she walks past me.

I put the blanket down. I go in the kitchen to get some food. My grandma's there in the hallway. She has her big straw hat on, rounded on top with the brim like an umbrella. Americans don't wear them. She's scared because the police came. I know she meant to go too if the police took me away. I tell her what happened.

"Berries?" she asks, not quite believing me. "Berries?" She can't understand that someone would call the police about berries. I shrug. Neither can I. "It's okay now," I say as I help her back to her room. "Don't worry."

"You buy berries, Du," she says. "All you want." She gives me money from her pocket to buy berries but it's Vietnamese money. She forgot. Then she adds, "This country has bad food but nice police." I don't tell her it has mean old men too. Everybody in the Philippines said, "America, America, it's a wonderful place, the best in the world." So Ba and Ma and Thuy and Lin and Vuong came here but the Americans wouldn't let my grandma and me come. That old spy didn't want us to come, I'm sure. Now maybe he wants to send us back so he spies and calls the police.

My dad comes home late like always. Thuy hurries to tell him about that old man spy calling the police about the berries. My dad slumps in the kitchen chair but his face sets into anger. "You stay in our yard from now on," he orders me. He goes to get something to eat. I make a face at Thuy. I guess I won't go out of the yard unless I get hungry and want some more berries. I don't care about staying in the yard. My dad'll forget about it anyway. He's too busy working to worry about a couple of berries. But that old man scared my grandma. I wonder if she worries we'll get sent back.

Later I take her tea and she tells me a story about a monkey in Vietnam who picked berries and when a snake bit him he thought it was a thorn from the berries so he didn't pay attention and the snake ate him. Usually in her stories I am a dragon, lordly and smart and powerful, not a stupid monkey. I laugh because we both know she's trying to teach me not to pick the berries.

● ● ●

I'm lying here thinking that some ripe berries would be very good for breakfast. It's so early that that old man is sure to be asleep. It's still mostly dark outside but I don't even need a light. I'll just toss my blanket in the closet, feel around for my clothes here on the floor, and I'm getting out of here.

It's nice outside in the time before morning. It's cool and quiet. Those berries must be fresh and wet from the dew. The old man's not even awake but I'll still go over the wall in back. It's so easy for me.

I'll just back up to get a run across the alley. Run. Jump as high as I can to grab the little crack in the blocks near the top. I strain with just my fingertips holding until my feet can find a rough spot to give me a boost up to the top. This is so easy. His big wall can't keep me out. It's easier than last time. I just reach over the top now and pull.

My hands flail around to get a grip but there's nothing to

hold on to, just slippery ooze all over the top. I'm going to fall. Oof! Ow! I can't breathe. I'm flat on my back in the alley gasping for breath and I know as soon as I can think that it's that old man who did it.

Finally I can pull some air into my lungs. I put my hand to my face and my hand is covered with black slippery oil. I look up at the top of the wall. At the end near our yard sits that cat, looking down at me. "Did you see that? He tried to kill me," I call to the cat.

I don't want anyone to see me lying on my back in this dumb alley. I thought I was dead but I can breathe now. I fell hard. I got black stuff all over my shirt and arms and hands. I hate that old man. He put that stuff there so I'd slip off his wall. I scraped my hand on the wall too, trying to grab something when I fell.

He thinks he saved his berries. No way. I'll just find something to put over that stuff. There's a lot of trash out today. Here's a box. Mash it down. Throw it on top of the wall. That's all.

Stupid cardboard won't stay up there. It's getting light out. I have to hurry before people start driving down the alley. There! It stuck. Now back up. Run, jump, pull. It's harder with this black stuff on my hands but I'm not going to let him stop me.

I'm on top but the cardboard is slippery. I can't reach many berries from up here. I'll just bend my knees and jump down into his yard.

Now what? I land with a splash in smelly stuff that stinks like a latrine and I almost lose my balance. What is this?

31

Yesterday his yard was all smooth green grass. Now there's smelly stinky water in a hole. Two traps that old man set for me. I don't want to fall over in this stuff. It's slippery and it's way over the top of my shoes. I hate that old man but he's a tricky old man, like the snake in my grandma's stories. Two traps when I thought he had only one. There's his kitchen light going on. I gotta get out of here. He'll think he won but I'm not going to forget. Two traps. My shirt and my arms are all covered with black stuff and my shoes are full of stinky water.

I throw away my shirt with all that black stuff on it, way down at the bottom of the garbage so my mom won't see it when she gets up. I put on another one but I only have three because she says that's all I need. I wear the same pants to school but they don't have so much stuff on them as the shirt. I wear my smelly shoes too because that's all I have. They're squishy with water and mud. The old man put dead fish or something in the water.

● ● ●

I'm early to school. Walking here I think of my grandma's story about the snake. There was a snake that kept trying to eat a turtle but it couldn't because of the turtle's hard shell. The snake thought it would be good if he had a hard shell too. He asked the turtle how he got his shell and the turtle said he got it by hitting himself over the head with a magic stick. The snake asked the turtle to hit him over the head with the stick because he, the snake, had no arms and couldn't do it himself. The turtle agreed. That's the end of the snake. The story's supposed to keep kids from being dumb and greedy like the snake but also to teach kids to be smart and tricky like the turtle. I'm a dragon but I like the tricky turtle too. I will be trickier than that old man.

I wait by the fence until the class lines up. I tag along at the end of the line so no one will hear the squishes or smell the smells. I washed but my arms and hands still have black stuff on them. I sit at my desk at the back hardly moving but it doesn't work. Anthony smells the fish smell.

"Hey, Du Du," he whispers. The others around me laugh. I know what *Du Du* is in American because I heard it before and asked Thuy. It sounds the same as dog doo-doo. "Hey, Du Du, your shoes are full of doo-doo," whispers Anthony again.

I jump up and crack him over the head with my note-book. "Shut up!" I yell. Suddenly everything is very quiet. Mrs. Dorfman looks at me through the top of her glasses. Her frizzy yellow hair makes her head look big. She stares at me so long that kids start to whisper. Some are laughing. I look down at my desk top. Mrs. Dorfman doesn't say anything. She gets out the pad of yellow slips. She writes so loud I can hear the writing. She tears the top sheet off. She waves it at me. *Squish, squish, squish.* I walk up the aisle. My smell goes all across the class. Everybody's whispering or giggling now. I take the yellow slip.

"Class, turn to page one hundred twenty-five," she says. Now she doesn't look at me at all. I go out the door. I take my time walking to the Counseling Center. I've been there four or five times already. The lady who runs it is Ms. Whipple. I remember because the first time I went Jorge told me she's called Ms. Whipple because she whips you. I was scared. Now I know she doesn't even yell at you. She just talks sadly about whatever you did. I don't look at her face but I know she's leaning forward trying to see inside me. I don't want her to. I look at her hands with bright pink nails twirling a pencil. Ms. Whipple points at a corner near the magazines when I come in. All the little cubicles are full. I like it better here than in class. It's more interesting. Big kids and little kids come in, angry or crying. I look at old magazines.

● ● ●

That night at home I run to answer the phone. I tell Ms. Whipple that my parents aren't home. True, but my grandma is. My grandma only knows about twenty words of English. I give her the phone. She says, "Yes, yes," every once in a while. Then she says, "Good-bye." This is easy. I'm glad my nosy sisters and brother are too busy reading their big fat books to ask what's going on.

My grandma looks at me. "Tell me, Du," she says in Vietnamese. I tell her about hitting someone at school. She's not satisfied. "Why?" she asks. I say he called me a name. "What?" she asks. I'm ashamed to tell her but she holds my sleeve and looks at me. I tell her how they change my name in English and what it means. I tell her they say I am dumb because I can't read. "Your name is Du," she says softly, "and

34

you are smart." She keeps hold of my sleeve. She goes to the kitchen and keeps me with her. I help her chop vegetables.

I don't tell my grandma about the old man and how he ruined my shirt and my shoes with his tricks. She will say, "You were the monkey and you weren't careful about the snake. You took his berries. Now you're even." But I don't think we're even. He called the police. My shirt's in the bottom of the garbage and my shoes still smell. And he's still a spy. Now what should I do to that old man to make it really even?

Tet-Trung-Thu

I look at the clock on the wall. Thirty-five minutes till lunch. Mrs. Dorfman has her deck of cards with our names on them. "Alan." She calls the name from the card. "What answer did you get for number fifteen, please?"

"Three and five-eighths," answers Alan.

"Did anyone get a different answer?" she asks. She frowns like he's wrong. He's right because that's the same answer I got. She fools a bunch of kids, though, who wave their hands around. "Rosaria," she says, and smiles, calling on one of the hands.

"I got fifteen," says Rosaria. Mrs. Dorfman does the whole problem on the overhead projector. This is going to take forever. I look around in my desk for something to do.

"So Alan was right." Mrs. Dorfman beams. "Now the answer for number sixteen, please, Du."

My paper's lost in a magazine I found in my desk. Everybody's waiting. I look sideways at Jorge's paper. "Four and three-tenths," I say.

"Speak up, Du," says Mrs. Dorfman. Then everybody laughs because that's what happens whenever she says my name. She wants me to say what I said again, only louder, but it's harder to hear with kids snickering and whispering "doo-doo," which the teacher also can't hear. Dumb Veronica starts telling Mrs. Dorfman what she thinks I said even though she doesn't know either.

"Shut up," I say. Then Mrs. Dorfman gets mad because she can hear that.

She sighs. She pulls out another card. "Jennifer, the answer to sixteen, please," she says. I find my paper. I got the right answer. I look at the clock. Twenty-six minutes until lunch.

I hate school. I'm not going to talk again until I can speak American like my brother and sisters. At least, I'm not going to talk at school.

In the cafeteria the lunch is ugly. It's cheese—stringy like snot—on mushy noodles, and chocolate milk, sickly sweet and not very cold. I eat the apple slices. I raise my hand to be excused to go to the playground. Veronica sits next to me because Mrs. Dorfman makes us walk in line.

Veronica says, "You gotta eat half before you can get up, Du." She says it loud enough for the lunch aide to hear. The lunch aide shakes her head at me—"No, you can't go yet"— and nods at my food—"Eat that first." I shrug and sit there.

Veronica's talking to the girl on her other side. I take my chocolate milk and pour it into Veronica's backpack. I stuff my cheesy mushy noodles into the empty milk carton. I raise my hand. The lunch aide nods—"Yes, you can go now"— and smiles happily at my empty tray. As I leave for the play-ground I hear Veronica shriek.

In the afternoon our class goes out to play softball. Mrs. Dorfman says to choose teams, boy, girl, boy, girl. I get cho-sen last. After the last girl. In the Philippines I was the one who chose the teams. We didn't play stupid softball there. We played kick-the-ball even though we had to make the ball from maybe an old tire or just trash tied in a bag. When no one was around to stop us we played throw-rocks-as-hard-as-you-can. Here Mrs. Dorfman sits on the bench and grades math papers. She looks up. "Don't throw the bat," she calls. In the field I stand with my hands in my pockets. When I'm up to bat the teacher watches. I sling the bat hard, almost to first base. "You're out, Du," she calls.

We're getting ready to go home. A boy from the smart kids' class brings a note for Mrs. Dorfman from the office. "Du," she calls above the noise. "You're to go to the office immediately."

"Oooh, Du, you're in trouble," kids whisper. I stroll slowly out of class. I pass Veronica on the playground on my way to the office. She is hurrying back to class with blurry eyes and a snotty nose. She doesn't look at me.

The principal calls me into his office. I stare at his tie. It has red and green giraffes on it. The principal points his finger at me. "Young man, you have not yet learned to respect other people's property." I don't say anything. "What shall we do about that?" His finger jabs the air. I'm pretty sure this is about Veronica but sometimes I think I did one thing and they say I did something else. I don't say anything. Why would anyone cry and tell the principal about milk in their backpack? Dump it out is what I would do. Then I'd pour some glue in the other guy's shoe.

The dumb giraffes, and thinking about shoe glue maybe, make me smile. The principal's hand slams down on his desk. "This is not a laughing matter." His voice is slow and angry. "You will have to pay for the young lady's three library books and her white sweater." I shrug. I don't have any money. "I will call your father to arrange for reimbursement." I don't know what that is but my stomach drops. My face stays the same, I hope. "Your rude attitude is only making this worse," he adds. Rude? I know what that means but I haven't even said anything.

"Look at me, young man," he commands. I look from the giraffes to his red face for only a second. Then I look at his shiny shoes. "Henceforth, you will eat in the detention corner." Good, I think, I won't have to sit next to Veronica. I have to get home fast to answer the phone. He waves me out but when I'm leaving he calls after me, "I will telephone your father at his place of employment." I'm not sure what he means. Then I'm mad at myself because he sees that I'm not sure and repeats himself. "I'm calling your father at work, young man. I have his number right here." He waves a white card around. There is no escape. My dad will be called at work and asked to pay.

I walk home slowly. Now I don't want to answer the phone. Not if it's my dad. When school first started he yelled at me about doing my homework but now he just yells at Thuy and Lin and Vuong if they're watching TV, not me. Now when he looks at me he sees my new clothes are messed up already. I know because he orders me to change but the other clothes don't look any better. He doesn't know that's the old man's fault.

Once I asked Vuong why Ba always looks so mad and yells at us for almost nothing. "I think it's because Mr. Vronsky, his boss, yells at him and he hates it so he yells at us," answered Vuong.

"That's not true," Lin butted in. "He yells at us so we'll work hard and be the best."

"Every time you cost him money means more time he has to work for Mr. Vronsky. He wants to have his own business where he's the boss," added Thuy. "Everyone can see that you don't work. You just mess around all the time. He hates that."

"I don't mess around," I said, and laughed at her. I grabbed her big eraser and her box of paper clips and her apple with the bite out of it. I tossed them into the air one at a

40

time and caught them until all three were going at once. I'm a good juggler.

"See!" Thuy shouted. "See what I mean."

I inched over to the window, still juggling, so if the old man was watching he could see a real show. I got the eraser and the paper clip box and the apple going really high until the paper clip box popped open and the paper clips flew everywhere. Thuy chased me until I tossed her her apple.

That was funny then but now I know, walking home, that what Lin said about my dad is true. He's angry because he doesn't think I work hard enough. I'm worried that he might be really angry this time. When I get home I think I'll try to fix the railing I broke on the front porch.

At home everything's the same so I forget to worry about my dad being angry. My grandma's sleeping. Thuy and Lin and Vuong are doing homework. I look out the window but the old man isn't spying now. He's probably opening cans of mushy American food to eat. I go outside to look for wood pieces for the railing. I mess around with some metal strips I find. I saw something called a catapult in the social studies book. I bet I could make one if I find some wood. I look in the alley. There's that gray cat I saw on the old man's wall. I wish she'd let me get close enough to pet her. She's even faster than me. She thinks I can't see her sleeping behind the trash cans.

I go out in front. Nothing's happening in any direction. The Mexican man isn't even fixing his truck or his car.

Screech, go somebody's tires. A car comes fast down the street. It's the same kind as my dad's. It is my dad's. Why's he coming home in the middle of the day? Then I remember. He's coming because of stupid Veronica. I go around in back quick. I go in the back door.

"Where's Du?" I hear him roar in the dining room. No one answers. From the doorway I see his face. His mouth is tight like a sealed box and his eyes are burning. He sees me. I look down. He lunges around the table where the others sit frozen. I'm so scared I run from him. I run around the table. He whacks at me from behind. The others duck out of the way. He knocks over the Buddha light.

"You bad boy! You lazy boy!" he shouts. I dive under the table. He kicks at me with his shoe but he misses me. I see my grandma's bare feet and the bottom of her black pants.

"Han, Han," she says softly. "He is your son."

The kicking stops. The room is very quiet but I still crouch under the table.

"It's all not worth it." His voice doesn't sound angry now that he's talking to my grandma. It sounds sad. "All the work is for nothing if the children go bad."

"They are not bad," murmurs my grandma. "Du is a good worker. He is new here."

"He doesn't work at school." My dad's voice is stronger now but not angry like before. "He does bad things. He is bad to the teachers. He throws away the money that we work for."

I look up from under the table. I can see the window. The old man spy is there, staring in, standing right in the

42

middle of his window. He saw me running and hiding. I hate him.

I see my dad's feet stalk out of the room. I hear the car screech away as he hurries back to work. I scramble out from under the table. Thuy and Lin and Vuong aren't quiet now. They all yell at me at once.

"Du, look what you did now. You're nothing but trouble."

"You're gonna be a gang boy if you act like that."

"You gotta act right at school."

"You start your homework right now." Lin takes a swipe at me as I go by the table but of course I get away and she's swiping the air.

I follow my grandma into the kitchen. She shakes her head sadly. She doesn't say anything at first. Neither do I. I am ashamed to tell her about Veronica and the backpack. She hands me a bowl of soup. "We waited a long time to come here and we came a long way, Du," she says softly.

"I know," I answer. I don't want to cry.

Later I tell Vuong how the principal said I was rude when I wasn't. "In America you gotta look at someone when they yell at you," he answers.

"Should I look at Ba?" I ask.

"No," he laughs. "No, I wouldn't do that if I were you." So the rule is: Look at angry Americans but don't look at angry Vietnamese. It's all a bunch of little stuff that doesn't matter. Americans stare at everything like that old man looking through our window. I wonder how much my dad has to pay for Veronica's stupid books and her ugly sweater. Maybe I'll make some money.

• • •

I don't care if they go to Orange without me. Thuy says it's a town like in Vietnam but I don't remember Vietnam either. I was too little when I left. My dad says I should stay home because he has to pay for Veronica's dumb library books but I know we wouldn't all fit in the car anyway. I'd be squished between Thuy and Lin and Vuong in the back and they'd be complaining about me. My dad would yell "Quit it" even though I wasn't doing anything. My grandma's sick so she needs to stay home anyway.

My parents take off work because it's Tet-Trung-Thu. They don't have it in America. It's for Vietnamese parents who work hard—to spend time with their children. Unless the children owe money for chocolate milk–covered library books, I guess. My family is going up to Orange overnight to stay with our cousins and do all the stuff you're supposed to do for this thing. We didn't do Tet-Trung-Thu while we were waiting in the Philippines. I'll ask my grandma. It's probably all dumb stuff anyway.

I'm not there when they go. They leave for Orange while I'm down the street watching the Mexican guy fix his truck. "Isn't that your car?" he asks when they drive by in our old Honda.

"Yeah," I say. I didn't think he knew anything about me. "They go to Orange for stuff with our cousins."

"What about you?" He looks at me.

"I'm taking care of my grandma." I watch while he scoots under the car.

"Hand me that wrench," he calls from under the car. Wrench? I don't want to ask him what that is. I hand him one of the tools. "Here, hold on to this." I reach down through the pipes. "See this thing?" he says. "Stick the wrench here and hold on tight."

I help him a long time. I remember my grandma when shadows come over the yard. "Gotta go. Bye," I say. I crawl out from under the car. I have black hands. My shirt has big smears of grease like my arms.

"Just you and that old lady with the hat?" he calls.

"Yeah, just us." I hurry home.

I run into the kitchen, where my grandma is making a cake for Tet-Trung-Thu. When she looks up and sees my shirt and hands she cries out, "Du, you wash." She says it crabby but I know she doesn't mean it. I scrub hard to get most of the grease off. My shirt stays dirty.

I know cooking's for girls but I like to break eggs and mix things and taste things. My grandma shows me how to break the eggs and pull the shells apart with only one hand. The other hand keeps mixing. I mess up at first so we eat scrambled eggs. Then we boil eggs and I eat the white part. The hard yolk we drop whole into the cake batter. We're making moon cake. The egg yolk looks like a moon when you slice it and you're lucky if you get it. They're probably having store-bought moon cake up in Orange. Those cakes aren't as good and they're not as lucky either.

We're waiting for the cake to cook so we make the lanterns. My grandma says that the lanterns show how bright the children are. For me, she says, we better make two extrabright ones. We don't have any bamboo but I find some sticks outside. We fold brown paper bags from the market in half and cut the slits for the light to shine through. My grandma shows me how to paste the sticks inside along the edges to make the lanterns strong. I use Lin's markers to make star and diamond designs on them while my grandma makes gold and green tissue paper strips from paper that came wrapped around fruit. We hang a candle holder from the sticks at the top. The candle has to be short or the lantern will burn up. They probably use flashlights up in Orange so they're safe, only one per kid.

My grandma tells me the story of the carp swimming in the muddy river who wanted to be a dragon ruling the earth so he worked and he worked and he studied and after a long time he was a dragon. I know why they tell this story. So kids'll work hard. It sounds so easy. I tell my grandma I'm already a dragon. She laughs and nods. "You are, you are," she says. We always talk in Vietnamese. The lanterns are finished. We eat the moon cake still warm. My grandma goes to take a nap.

Later in the dark we take the lanterns outside. We light both of them at once. I start leaping around with them so the shadows dance all around me. My grandma watches from the steps. I bet that old man's watching from his window. He thinks I'm crazy. He thinks I'm going to burn the yard up, and both our houses. I jump higher. I act crazier just for him.

● ● ●

I'm sitting on the front steps. I see two guys from my school ride by on bikes. I yell but they don't stop. I don't think they heard me. I wonder where they go. I see my dad's car down the street coming back from Orange. He stops in the street. My mom and Thuy and Lin and Vuong get out. My dad drives off. The others come up the walk and into the house with their bags. They walk slowly like me when I go to my dumb kids' reading group. Vuong sits down at the worktable with his books. He's the best one to ask about things.

"Where'd Ba go?" I ask. My dad didn't even wave, he was in such a hurry to go.

Vuong shrugs. "He's all worried about missing work. Ma had to give lots of money to her sister for her uncle's medicine. We all sat around and did a bunch of corny stuff with lanterns. I had to sleep in the car because it was too crowded in the house. It took hours to get back and the car started to smoke." Vuong looks at me like he is daring me to laugh. I want to tell him how we made delicious sweet cake and I got the lucky moon and how I danced like a crazy guy until the lanterns burned up and I had to jump up and down on them to keep the weeds from burning. I don't because I feel bad about the money again.

My mom comes to the doorway. "Vuong, you come with me," she orders. She's yanking a comb through her hair with one hand and buttoning her coat with the other. "They've got extra work tonight."

"I'm not sewing!" Vuong almost shouts at her. "Sewing's for girls. Make Thuy and Lin go."

"They've got too much studying," answers my mom. She gives up easier than my dad. She looks sad now.

"Me too," says Vuong.

Money! I think. I could make money to pay for Veronica's stuff. "I'll go!" I jump up.

"You can't do it. You're too young." A car honks outside. It's her ride. She turns to leave.

"I can, I can. Ask grandma." I run after her.

"Oh, come," she says as she opens the door. She stops to look right into my eyes. "You be good, Du. No tricks or you'll be sorry." I nod because I know I'll be good. I'll make enough money to pay for the library books and her uncle's medicine.

I am in the car with five women all talking Vietnamese at once. I am crouched on the floor so the police won't stop us for the seat belt law. I am squished. It is a long trip.

We finally get to the sewing place, which is in somebody's big garage. Sewing machines and chairs are shoved together in crooked rows with boxes of cloth at the front of the rows. Women are already working. My mom sits me down at a machine and leans over me to show me fast how to sew. I pay attention. I'm helping to make Christmas stockings with just two lines of sewing, up one side and down the other. Then I give them to the lady behind me to do something else. We get paid for how many we finish. My mom hurries off to talk to the lady in charge so I start to do what she showed me. She sits down across the room in another row of machines. When I press the the pedal the machine taps its way down one side of the stocking. It's fun. All I can hear are sewing machines and women speaking Vietnamese. It's easy.

"No good!" yells the lady behind me. She throws the red stocking at my head. "He's no good for this."

My mom runs over. "Sorry, sorry." She bows to the lady. She looks at the bad stocking. She shows me how it's wrong. She leans across me to do a stocking on my machine. "There," she says. "Like that." As she straightens up I see her eyes. They plead with me. I bend my head close to watch the line on my next stocking. I make it straight.

I do ten stockings, twenty, fifty. It's not fun. It's boring, boring. My neck feels stiff and crooked. I glance ahead of me. There are boxes of stockings taller than me at the start of the line. I remember my mom's eyes. I sew more lines and I watch each one closely. I will not let that lady behind me yell again.

I look up later and only one box is gone. I quit looking. Now my neck *and* my shoulders have little prickles of pain in them but I stop thinking about it. I watch the lines of stitches across the red cloth. Over and over again. Once my mom comes over to show me how to replace the thread that comes up from the bottom. After that I do it myself. The boxes empty so slowly.

Women stand up around me. They talk quietly now. I let myself look up. All the piles of boxes from the front of the line are gone. I am so tired. We close the machines and leave.

Everyone in the car is quiet now so I fall asleep on the floor. My mom wakes me up when we're at our house. It's very dark. "Come," she says. She pulls me out of the car. I am still almost asleep. "You are a good boy," she whispers as we let ourselves into the quiet house. "A good worker." I fall down on the couch in my clothes and go back to sleep.

I don't sleep very long before my dad shakes me awake. "Get up," he commands. "We gotta go." With my dad I don't ask. I get up. I stagger out the door after him and get in the car. I am asleep before he reaches the end of our block. I don't know where we're going.

When he shakes me again it is just beginning to be light. Where are we? I'm so tired. I drag after him across a street. I wait almost sleeping on my feet while he talks to a man. We get in a different car and drive away. "We'll get home in time for school," he says. I fall asleep.

This time when I feel the car stopping I wake myself up. We are home. "Hurry up, lazy boy," my dad says as he rushes ahead of me into the house. Inside, when I look at the clock, I know school has already started. I grab my backpack before I head for the door.

My mom comes out of the bedroom like she just woke up. My grandma comes from the kitchen. "Where have you been with him?" my mom asks. She sounds worried.

"I heard about a better car for us from Van. I wanted to

get it fast so I took Du." He took me so he could drive in the diamond lane. He needs two people to drive there. "He's a lazy boy. He just sleeps," adds my dad scornfully. My mom and grandma both talk at once. My mom tells him how I sewed as good as anyone with all of us working until two in the morning. She tells him I made money. My dad was gone when we went to sew so he didn't even know I went with her. Her voice is high and loud.

He stands quiet for a few moments before he starts to laugh. "So not such a lazy boy," he laughs. "I'll drive you to school." I've never been driven to school. "I'll tell your teacher why you're late."

"He eats first." Now it is my grandma's turn with her soft voice. She gives me rice and vegetables. I eat fast standing up.

My dad mutters "lazy boy" and laughs some more when he drives me to school. But I know he is laughing at himself, not me.

He walks with me to my class. Mrs. Dorfman looks up when we are standing in the door. Her mouth is tight like she ate a lemon. "Yes?" she says. The class is quiet because they want to hear what's happening.

"Du late. He has work to do for his family. Important work." I don't know the right English but I know how he says it is not right. I look down. I wait for the snickers of laughter. I clench my fist. "School is important," he says. "Du not late again." He walks across the class to Mrs. Dorfman's desk. I look up. He is smiling. He does not bow. He holds out his hand like an American. She struggles quickly

51

out of her chair to shake his hand. She is smiling. The class is quiet. In one minute they know they can't laugh at my dad. There is something important about him even with his bad English. Mrs. Dorfman doesn't say "Go to the office." She smiles and nods politely as he leaves. "Du, we're on page twenty-two in spelling," she says kindly. I sit down. I'm still tired but I'm happy. I'm a kid who does important stuff for his family.

The next morning I ask my mom if I can sew again. She looks quickly over at my grandma. "You were very good, Du. You learned so quickly and you kept up with everybody," she answers. "But you are too young. It is better for you to do your schoolwork." My grandma smiles a little smile at the stove.

The Trap

There are ghosts in America too. I'm trying to sleep but I can hear them outside in the dark, moaning and yowling. My grandma tells me stories about ghosts in Vietnam but Thuy and Lin and Vuong laugh. They say there aren't any ghosts in America. The reading teacher read a story about a ghost at school. In the picture it looked like a little kid with a sheet on and big eyes and it didn't do anything bad but it was a ghost. The kind that are outside making all that noise sound more like the ones in Vietnam. The ghosts there come for revenge because something bad happened when they died. I can't sleep. I wonder if anyone else can hear them. I wonder if they ever come inside.

That's a car door slamming. The ghosts stop moaning. It's very quiet. Footsteps on the front porch stairs. For a moment I'm scared. Stupid me. My mom is coming home from work. "Hi," I say when she opens the door.

"Why are you awake?" she grumbles like she's mad but I know she isn't. She doesn't sleep so good either. Sometimes we meet each other walking around the house in the dark. Thuy says she's thinking about her family left behind in Vietnam. I'm just thinking about all kinds of stuff.

"Do you hear anything?" I ask. I don't want to say ghosts because I don't want her to know I'm afraid. I think she believes in ghosts too, at least in Vietnam. She sits on the end of the couch. She holds my foot through the blanket while we listen.

"There," I whisper. The moaning has started again. I feel her hand grip tighter. We scarcely breathe, listening.

She shakes my foot. I hear a smile in her voice. "It's just cats," she whispers. "There's a cat outside with some boyfriends." I laugh but very quietly.

"I've seen the cat on the wall," I say. "She's big and gray and from the way they're yowling she's got a lot of big loud boyfriends." I laugh at myself for being afraid of cats. That's what the darkness does to me sometimes.

Slowly my mom gets to her feet. Ever since I went sewing with her I can feel myself how tired she is. "You go to sleep now," she says.

"You go to sleep too," I whisper. I lie awake for a little while listening to the wild sad sound of the cats.

• • •

I hate school. Veronica waves her hand around to remind Mrs. Dorfman it's time for my superdumb reading group in Room 10. When I get up to leave I step on Veronica's toe because her foot's sticking out in the aisle. "Ouch!" she yells as though it really hurt. Mrs. Dorfman gives us both a mean look. When I get to Room 10 we read a story about some ants who yell "Hooray!" because they're going on a picnic. I used to squash ants too. I wonder if they yelled "Ouch!" when I squashed them. The teacher puts a big white paper up on her easel. "Who can tell us something they know about ants?" she asks, and smiles. I don't say anything. I think about that old man. My dad saw the hole in my pants this morning and the black oily stains on them and he was mad.

"Clothes cost money!" he shouted. He doesn't even know about my shirt in the trash and my smelly shoes.

"Du, I'm sure you know something about ants," says the teacher. "Can you tell us?"

"They kill chickens," I answer.

The teacher says just what I knew she'd say. "Oh, Du, I don't think that's true." I know it's true because it happened to some chickens in the Philippines. Big red ants swarmed all over them and killed them but she doesn't even know about that.

When I get back to class Mrs. Dorfman has been talking too much. I can tell by the way everybody looks up fast when I open the door as though they hope they're going to be rescued. Anthony has his big mouth open in a yawn. I'm glad I didn't have to sit through it. "Writing Assignment: Write four paragraphs about a favorite pet" is written on the board.

"If you don't have a pet," says Mrs. Dorfman, looking at me, "write about an imaginary pet or a pet you'd like to have." But American kids have pets and I'm going to have a pet too. I'm going to catch that gray cat.

• • •

I need just the right box for my cat trap. Down here by the market is where they have the best ones. Strong ones that canned stuff comes in. I have to duck. There are two kids from school. If they see me here they'll call me a trash picker. Here's a great box with double cardboard. No cat could get out of it.

Now I've got wood for the trigger I have to carve. I have to make it very smooth with just the right curve or it won't work. When she goes in to get the food her weight will pull on the trigger just enough to move the prop stick and make the door fall down. I'll glue on a piece of brick to make it fall harder and make it stay shut. A cat can't move a brick. I'll put it together in the yard where the old man can see me from his window. He'll worry about what I'm doing. I saw guys carving triggers like this in the Philippines but they were catching monkeys and lizards. Lizards are dumb but monkeys are smarter than cats so I think this trap will work. I need some bait that a cat will really love.

"I'm gonna take this fish head, okay?" My grandma nods.

"What do you want that stinky thing for?" Lin always has to know what I'm doing so she can say I shouldn't do it.

"I'm gonna make a sandwich," I answer.

"You can't make a sandwich out of that. It's got eyes and bones—"

"Hush, Lin," interrupts my grandma. She smiles and puts her hand on Lin's arm. I take the fish head outside. I balance the lid of the box on the stick with the trigger curved around it. It falls easily, which is good, until I balance it just right. I put it way in the back of the yard so the old man can't see. He might let my cat go just to be mean. He might even kill it.

I go inside and watch the trap from the back window. Nothing happens. I'm getting bored so I catch a fly in my fist to put in a spiderweb but then I let it go. The fly's happy to be free. When I look up that old man is carrying a little blue bowl across his yard to the shed. He puts it down on the ground and goes slow like a turtle back inside. I run out and look over the side fence. It's fish from a can. He's been watching the whole time. He's trying to stop me from catching that cat. Well, any cat would rather have a fresh fish head than fish from a can. I'll catch her.

● ● ●

It's getting light out. I'll go out quick and check my trap. When I catch the cat I'll find something else for her to eat and shut her up someplace where no one will find her.

It's still pretty dark out here and the grass is wet.

The trap door is down! I caught her! I caught her in one day. I'll have to be careful she doesn't get away when I lift the box. I'll hold the lid tight and turn it over carefully so I don't hurt her.

That cat smells. She smells like a skunk.

Ugh, I caught a skunk. It's not very big and it's all curled up in there. I know my mom and dad won't let me keep it. They won't even let me keep a cat.

Maybe the old man would like a pet. He gave me smelly shoes so maybe he'd like a smelly skunk. I could put it down the chimney but then it might get stuck in there or get hurt. I'll put it in the mailbox. I'll put up the little flag. He'll reach his hand in there and, *whoosh*, he'll smell worse than my shoes ever did. I think I can do it without getting sprayed.

I'll grab it out of the box in a towel and keep its tail down so it can't spray. I'll stuff it backward into the mailbox and I'll run.

Okay, little skunk. Don't be afraid. I'm just gonna wrap you up nice in this towel.

Hey, don't try to get away. I'm not gonna hurt you. Keep your tail down.

Poor little skunk, you're shaking. You're scared I'm going to kill you. You've got a cute face. I bet you miss your family. I wonder if that old man will kill you. He probably will.

I can't do that to you, little skunk. I won't. Stop shaking. I'll take you someplace safe. Did you get caught in my trap and lose your family? I'll take you to the place where they knocked the old house down. You'll find a hole to hide in and I've seen worms there after a rain. You can eat them. There are lots of garbage cans too. You don't smell so bad. I don't think so, anyway.

Okay, this is the place. I'll put you down near a hole and I'll run. I know you're still scared enough to spray me. I hope you find your family. I hope I see you again.

•   •   •

"What's that awful smell?" Thuy covers her mouth and nose with her hands when I go inside for something to eat.

"Du, you stink! Get out of here!" Lin and Vuong yell, and cover their noses. I go to the sink. My dad in his underwear comes from the hallway. He was still sleeping because he didn't come home until the middle of the night.

"Du, you stupid!" He grabs me by the neck. He shoots me out the back door. He throws the soap from the sink out after me. "You come in when you don't smell," he yells. Thuy's flapping a towel around in the kitchen behind him. I go to the faucet on the side of the house. Water dribbles out. I know I'll still smell when I go to school.

I don't care if I got in trouble even though I was just trying to get a pet so I could do Mrs. Dorfman's writing assignment. I'm glad I let the skunk go. He'll be happy down by that hole where no one lives. Maybe he'll find his family. I know skunks live there because a kid at school told about seeing them.

I still need a pet. Maybe I won't catch the cat but I'll feed her and make friends with her. That's the same as a pet.

Open House

"Boys and girls, we all know about our special event this week," announces Mrs. Dorfman. I don't know about any special event but I listen because maybe it will be better than the regular stuff.

"Open House is Thursday!" she announces. Open House? I wonder if she will open her house. Or worse, make me open my house. It sounds dumb. "We'll have our very best work out for our parents to see." She pauses with a big smile. So *open house* is really *open school* with parents coming. I don't have any "best work" or even much work at all.

"We'll present a wonderful program for our parents in class." Pause. I know I won't be in any program. "We'll join the whole school for delicious refreshments in the cafeteria with a welcome from Mr. Martin." I quit listening because my parents don't have time to come to this stuff.

We decorate our folders for Open House while she hands out a bunch of our work she's saved to put in them. We get our last math test. I got two wrong because they were dumb problems. One was "Find the product of 58 and 17." I don't know *product* but I thought it sounded more like *subtract* than any of the others so I subtracted. I subtracted right. The other problem was about a bunch of American kids who give away one third of their marshmallows and then a half of what's left but I couldn't figure out which kid had them in the first place. They had funny names and I don't know what marshmallows are. Birds, I think. Anthony shoves his math test in a book in his desk because it's all covered with red marks.

"Anthony put his test in his desk," cries Veronica.

"The test goes in your folder, Anthony," says Mrs. Dorfman as if he doesn't know. "Make your desks nice and tidy for desk inspection," she says. My desk is messy. I put my rubber bands in my pocket so she doesn't take them. I look up. Anthony hits Veronica in the back of the head with a marker cap. She rubs her head like it really hurts. She turns around with her face all squished up. Anthony points at me. Veronica raises her hand to tell. "Would you pass out our personal narratives for me, please, Veronica?" Veronica forgets about complaining. She's so happy handing out our writing stuff and looking at everybody's grade. She drops mine on my desk like it's dirty. "Du" I wrote in big scrawled letters at the top. Then "My Summer Vacation" written even bigger. Then nothing. I wrote it my second day at American school because she wouldn't let me go to recess until I turned in "something." Mrs. Dorfman wrote U at the top, which means *Unsatisfactory*.

Tiffany passes out the markers. She gives me a bad box with mostly purple ones with the tops off. I decorate my folder as fast as I can. I make a stick guy who's throwing a bunch of marker tops at another stick guy, who's Anthony. Melissa passes out spelling tests. I have another U because I quit right in the middle. It was boring. No one's going to see my folder anyway.

Damian passes out letters for our parents about the Open House. I fold mine into a little box. In the Philippines we made boxes like this to fill with water and throw. But we didn't have much paper. Here I could throw boxes all day with the junk paper in my desk. Tiffany sees it and asks how to do it. I toss it to her as we go out the door to go home.

● ● ●

"Du, your Open House is tomorrow. I'll tell Ba and Ma." Thuy is opening the mail.

"No," I yell, trying to grab the letter. It's no fair for the school to send a letter too.

She holds it over her head. I jump and grab it. I ball it up and throw it at Vuong across the table because he's reading

63

too much. He pushes his chair over to chase me. I see the old man looking at us through his window. Vuong gives me a little swat on the back. For the old man I act like he's trying to murder me. I fall across the table. I let my tongue hang out and roll my eyes to give the old man a good show. Lin yanks her book out from under my head.

"What's a marshmallow?" I call back as I leave to watch TV. They all talk at once to show they know. It's food you put on a stick and burn. Fun! Maybe I'll buy a box of marshmallows someday.

● ● ●

"Du, you meet me at Fortieth Street at the bus stop at six-fifty. You be there."

My mom is coming to the Open House. Thuy told her she should go to find out about my schoolwork. My mom drives to work in a car with a bunch of other women but today she's coming home early on the bus. I told her it would be dumb but she's coming anyway. My dad is too busy.

● ● ●

It's strange to be at school at night. Lights from the classrooms shine out on the dark playground. Kids are running around all over. Mrs. Dorfman's in a shiny dress instead of pants. She even cleaned her coffee cup. My mom sits at my desk. Tiffany's mom and dad sit at her desk squashed together with her little brother sitting on her work folder. All

64

the kids in our class sit on the floor in the front. We look right at Mrs. Dorfman's legs. Kids giggle. The room gets crowded so people even stand around the edge. It's very hot. I turn to look at my mom. She has room to sit at my desk by herself. She is sitting straight and smiling. I look at Anthony's desk. Is that his mom? She doesn't look old enough to be a mom. She wears jeans and a T-shirt and lots of makeup under her big old glasses. She is busy looking at Anthony's folder. It has a guy with fangs drawn on the front. She doesn't look happy.

"I'm glad so many of our wonderful parents could make it to Open House." Mrs. Dorfman smiles. I'm close enough to know she smells like old flowers. I wiggle around to get more room. I bump Anthony. He doesn't do anything back. He just sits there staring straight ahead. "I'm going to tell you some things about our class and about my expectations for my students . . ."

Oh no, I think. This is going to last forever. I twist around. Moms and dads are all smiling back. My mom too. Little kids are already squirming around.

I'm right, of course. On and on she talks. It's very hot. She smiles and smiles. Jorge starts opening and closing the Velcro on his shoes. She beams down at him like he's doing something wonderful. "Let's not play with our Velcro, boys and girls," she whispers. Anthony doesn't even laugh.

Mrs. Dorfman calls kids to stand up in front to tell about reading and math and spelling and social studies. I twist around. I can tell who their moms and dads are by who's smiling biggest. Kids come up to read their poetry about rain. Kids come up to tell about the class newsletter and computer time. It's only fun to see how scared they are. "Speak up," Mrs. Dorfman keeps saying. "Speak up, please."

I twist around again. Oh no! My mom looks funny. Her head drops forward and jerks back. Is she going to sleep? I look up and down the row of sitting kids to see if anyone saw. "Sleepyhead" is what Mrs. Dorfman called Rosaria when she went to sleep in class. I can just hear Anthony and Jorge. "How's Son of Sleepyhead?" they'll say. Then they'll snore.

I sneak another look. My mom's asleep. Her head's propped up on her hand. Her eyes are closed. I can't hear if she's snoring because of Mrs. Dorfman. On and on and on. I don't look anymore. If I don't look maybe nobody else will. If Anthony laughs at her I'll jump up and smash him. I don't care who's here. My mom works late every night. She's tired. I'm listening carefully now for one kid who says one thing about my mom.

Finally Mrs. Dorfman sounds like she's through. "I think that covers everything now." She is as smiley and loud as when she started. Maybe she doesn't see my mom. "Are there any questions?"

A loud angry voice. "You bet there are!" All the kids twist around. It's Anthony's mom. She's standing up at his desk. She's glaring at Mrs. Dorfman. "I thought this was supposed to be a democracy," she shouts. "How come just some of the kids are up there talking? I didn't come here to hear somebody else's kid and how great they're doing. I got other stuff to do."

The room is very quiet. "I'm sorry you're disappointed," says Mrs. Dorfman, still smiling but not as much. "It was a volunteer—"

"Whatever," interrupts Anthony's mom. "I hope you know you graded this math paper wrong also." She waves Anthony's red-marked math test in the air. "I don't know how you expect the kids to do it when you can't even do it." Next to me Anthony is staring at the floor. I look back at his mom. This is interesting. My mom is awake, looking surprised.

"I'll be happy to talk to you privately," answers Mrs. Dorfman, who is finally not smiling. "The rest of you might like to go to the cafeteria for refreshments and to hear a welcome from our principal." Chairs scrape. Kids jump up except Anthony. Everyone talks at once. Anthony's mom stalks to the front of the room.

"Time to go home," I say to my mom. She doesn't know about the cafeteria or doesn't care. We go out through the playground gate.

"Your teacher is very nice," she says.

"She's boring," I answer. "You went to sleep."

"You be nice, Du," my mom says in her strict voice. I hear under her strict voice that she is trying not to laugh.

"Is it nice to go to sleep when the teacher's talking?" I laugh. She can't help it. She laughs too.

"So much English at once sounds to me like beautiful music," she murmurs. "I woke up when that mother yelled. For a moment I thought I was back in Vietnam and the teacher would hit my fingers with a ruler."

"What?" I laugh. "She wouldn't do that!" My mom was dreaming the teacher would hit her. This is so funny.

"In Vietnam when I was little this is what happened when I fell asleep in school," she answers.

"You fell asleep in your school in Vietnam?" I almost don't believe her. Vietnam is so far and strange that I can't even imagine real things happened there. "And the teacher hit you with a ruler?"

"Yes," she laughs. "And another time when I brought a little frog to school."

"You took a frog to school?" This is great. I want to know. We stop for a red light. Her face looks distant now, not laughing.

"That was a long time ago," she says. "We're here now." I'm disappointed because I know she won't say anything else. When she remembers something fun or happy in Vietnam, I think it must always lead to something sad; then she won't talk anymore. I would like to know but I don't want to make her sadder by asking.

● ● ●

"We had a wonderful Open House," announces Mrs. Dorfman the next day. "Now it's time to get back to work." Anthony sits angry at his desk, daring anyone to say anything. I wonder what happened with his mom and Mrs. Dorfman after we left. Tiffany brushes her little brother's cracker crumbs off her desk. No one says anything about how my mom went to sleep. I don't think they even know. I saw my mom sitting at the dining room table in the middle of the night when I got up to get a drink. She was looking at the Buddha and the pictures. I know she was thinking about Vietnam.

In the Shed

I hope that old man doesn't come home while I'm in here. It's his shed, even though the side with the little window is right on the edge of our yard. What if he caught me stuck there in the little window like I was when I climbed in? He'd have to be in our yard to see my legs kicking around high up in the air trying to get me through. If he unlocked the shed door he'd see my head and arms waving around stuffed in that window like a ghost up in the air. Maybe he'd be scared. If I saw him like that I'd think it was funny but I don't think he knows how to laugh. But he only comes in here for his lawn mower and that's only on Tuesday. He won't see the window because he can only see that from our yard. That's why he boarded it up, I bet. He didn't want us looking in at his stuff. There's nothing here that anybody would want anyway. There's his lawn mower right by the door. It's as old as he is. He's always fixing his yard, making it look better than everybody else's. He doesn't do any work except mow that lawn. My dad's got more important stuff to do. He has to work to make money. My mom too. Then maybe we'll hire that old man to mow our lawn. I'll sit on the steps and drink a soda and point to the spots he misses.

Here are his tools. My dad says Americans all have tools but they can't fix anything. I'm gonna fix that old man's lawn mower for him. His lawn should look just like everybody else's around here. I won't take it all apart. I'll just loosen all these places so it falls apart when he pushes it. He'll think it just got so old it died. It's easy to loosen these bolts because he oils it so much.

I wonder what else is in here. I think my cat has a way to get in. When she comes for the fish or other stuff I give her she often comes running from the back of the shed. I hope the old man doesn't hurt her if he finds her inside. I better get out. It wasn't very smart of him to put this old trunk here so I could climb back out the window easier. I wonder what's in it.

A lot of old junk is what's in it. I'll make sure there's nothing good at the bottom. Old toys. This little truck is so heavy. I wonder if that old man played with a truck. Can it be that old? Here's a football and a baseball and bat. I have to be careful so I can remember where all this stuff goes back. The whole bottom's covered with boxes. They could have good stuff in them. I'll come back later. He just went walking down the street. I don't want to be stuck in that window when he gets back. I'll fix the plywood back over it just like it was.

• • •

"Boys and girls, today we're going to be authors again. We're going to write another personal narrative piece for our portfolios." Everybody groans. On the overhead projector Mrs. Dorfman puts a big plastic page with "Personal Narrative" in fancy writing. She covers up the bottom part. Then she talks and talks and talks. I look at car pictures in a magazine I found on the rack in the Counseling Center. I read it in my lap so Mrs. Dorfman and Veronica can't see it. Anthony's squirming around trying to shoot a mini-skateboard over to Jorge with his foot.

"And the subject will be . . ." Mrs. Dorfman stops in midsentence. I look up. She's waving her pencil around like something wonderful is about to happen. She uncovers more of the writing on the projector. "Write About a Family Journey," it says. She reads it in a loud excited voice. There's a picture of an American family waving from their car. Kids who usually write stuff raise their hands. "We wrote about that already," someone blurts. That's what Mrs. Dorfman calls it when you just yell something without getting called on. I'm not a blurter because I don't talk. Sometimes Mrs. Dorfman makes the blurter stand up and apologize to the class. This blurter doesn't get in any trouble.

"Relax, relax." She smiles. "All your questions will be answered in due time."

"Du Du time," whispers Anthony. Jorge laughs. I kick the mini-skateboard down the aisle.

"Paragraph one will be about where your family planned to go and why you decided to go there. It doesn't have to be a vacation. We're writing about the journey, there and back, and the destination, what we did there. Does anyone have a good idea he or she can share?" Kids raise their hands. One kid says, "We went to La Mesa on the bus." Some kids snicker. I don't know why.

Alan raises his hand in the front of the room. "We rented a RV to go to Carlsbad Beach for my brother's birthday," he says.

"Wonderful! That's a story," says Mrs. Dorfman, smiling. She talks again about paragraphs and stuff like that.

Mrs. Dorfman smiles at the hand-raisers. "Those are wonderful ideas, boys and girls." She pulls the sheet on the overhead down so we can see another line. "Paragraph two will be about the trip itself. Did you enjoy it? How did you pass the time? How did you think about your destination— where you were going?

"Paragraph three. Describe your destination, the place to which you went. Tell about your activities. What did you do there?" Mrs. Dorfman's talking faster now because almost everyone's yawning and wiggling around in their seats. Not just me. Her voice is getting louder. "Paragraph four." She forgets to uncover the last line. She's staring at Jorge. He's leaning into the aisle to get back the mini-skateboard. Angela won't let him have it. She moves it with her foot just when he almost grabs it. Angela's in the high reading group.

Suddenly everybody looks up. We are all interested. A little bug is walking across the overhead projector over the words. Kids elbow each other and whisper. Mrs. Dorfman doesn't know. She looks confused for a moment. Her eyes sweep across the room and land on me. She thinks I'm messing around. A good kid tells her about the bug. She squishes it with a tissue. Her voice is sharp now. "Write about the trip home and how you feel about your trip. Would you like to go back? Any questions? . . . Put on the proper heading. Let's get started." Mrs. Dorfman shuts off the overhead.

"How long do the paragraphs have to be?"

"What if we never went anyplace?"

"Is this a rough draft?"

"What are we supposed to do?" Kids are blurting questions from all over the room. Jorge snatches the mini-skateboard from under Angela's foot.

"Write a personal narrative," snaps Mrs. Dorfman. "Anyone who does not have a rough draft of at least two pages will stay after school. No talking." I look down at my magazine, where there's a picture of a blue truck with big wheels and lightning bolts on the side. Then I remember. It's Tuesday. I want to be there to laugh when that old man goes out to mow and his old mower falls apart all over his nice green grass. I rip a piece of paper off my pad. I write "Du" at the top. I write my personal narrative. "I went to Disneyland. I went with my mom and dad and brother and sisters. We went in the car. It was fun. I saw people dressed like big mice. I went on rides. I ate lots of food. I would like to go again." Mrs. Dorfman is walking up and down the aisles. She taps her finger on my paper. "Good job, Du," she says. I've never been to Disneyland.

Anthony and Jorge have to stay after school but I get to go even though my personal narrative was just a little bit of one page. I run. I see that the old man hasn't mowed his grass yet. I get an apple and a banana. I look out the back window, where I can see the shed. Now I'm the spy. Finally he comes out his back door. He's so slow. He stoops over to pick up a little bit of nothing on his grass. He puts it in his shirt pocket. He looks over at our yard. I bet it was something that blew over there from our yard because we never mow. Our yard's full of high weeds and tall brown grass that hides rusty tools and cracked pots people left there long ago. Some places you can hardly walk. That's why the cat is my cat. She hunts in my yard. I see her crouched low and silent with just her tail twitching and I've seen a lizard tail out there and bird feathers she left in the shaggy bushes in back. In the old man's yard she'd never catch anything.

At the shed the old man tips the lock this way and that, trying to see. He does everything like slow-motion stuff on TV. I just want to see that mower fall apart. The door is open. Here comes the mower. It's just out of the shed when the first wheel falls off. He doesn't see it. He thinks it's stuck on something so he gives it a big hard push. He's standing there holding the handle and the rest of the mower is in a mess on the ground. I burst out laughing. He looks at it with his mouth puckered up. Then his head stays still but his eyes under his bushy eyebrows move toward my window. I duck. I wait a few minutes. I look again. He's not there. Just that old pile of lawn mower parts. He's probably calling 911. He can't prove anything. I go away to watch TV.

"What are you laughing about?" asks Lin from the dining room. She's in there even more than Thuy and Vuong now, taking care of some plants she grew like they were little babies.

"Nothing." I shrug. It's so funny I wish I could tell somebody but not Lin. She doesn't like anything I do.

Cartoons are over. I go look out the window again. There he is. He's made a table with some old boards. He has the lawn mower parts up on the table with a bunch of rags and oil and wrenches. He's kind of whistling, putting the lawn mower back together. He's sharpening the blades. I wish I could watch up close.

I go outside. I pretend I'm washing my feet at the outside faucet. I don't look at him but I look around for my cat. I see her on the roof of the shed. "Hey, Cat, come here," I say in Vietnamese. She's fat now because I feed her every day. I hope she doesn't get so fat she can't run from the old man.

"You better leave that cat alone," the old man calls. "She could have rabies." I shrug. I don't know what that is but I won't ask him.

"You left the water on," he says when I walk away, like he's telling me what to do. He can't tell me what to do.

"Your mower broke?" I ask as if I didn't know.

"I'm just doing some maintenance," he says. "You'd need a scythe to cut that yard of yours." I don't know what *maintenance* is and I don't know what *scythe* is. I go inside. I slam the door. Later I ask Thuy about *rabies* and *maintenance* and *scythe*. I know my cat doesn't have rabies. I hope he's not trying to catch her so they can kill her. She's too smart for him to catch her anyway. It would be fun to have a scythe and go swinging it all over the yard.

I swing a pretend scythe a few times but Thuy and Lin and Vuong keep reading. I swing it over near the window, where all of Lin's science experiment plants are lined up in their little pots. Lin keeps her head down in her book. This is odd. I make a whooshing sound and take a few more swings at the plants. I come as close as I can but I don't have a real scythe so I don't hurt them. Lin jumps up. Her eyes are red. Tears stream down her face.

"Knock them over! Throw them out! It doesn't matter," she cries. She runs out of the room.

"What'd I do?" I protest before Thuy and Vuong can yell at me too.

"You're teasing her and she's already heartbroken," Thuy answers.

"Why?" This is interesting. The plants looks fine. All exactly alike and about five inches tall in their little matching pots. I didn't hurt them.

"As if you care!"

"I care," I argue. I would care if something bad happened to Lin but why would she cry about little plants?

"Lin cares about school. Unlike one of us," Thuy answers scornfully. She means me, of course. "She's in a special Young American Scientist program and the plants are for her science project. She's supposed to find mutant speed-seed plants and then she grows more and more until they're all mutants."

77

I don't know about speed-seed plants but I know about mutants from TV. They're usually giant blobs with crooked teeth and noses and their hands growing out of their foreheads. I shrug. I can see from the cute little plants that she doesn't have any mutants. "So?" I say.

"So?" Vuong mimics me. "So she doesn't have any mutants and the first part of the experiment is due tomorrow. She did all that work and wrote the report and now she won't have time to start growing them again and finish on time."

"How about finish late?" I suggest. How much difference can it make?

Thuy stands up with her hands on her hips to argue. "She can't be in the science project class if she doesn't keep to the schedule and have a project to turn in. And Lin cares. She wants that more than anything."

They're both acting like somehow it's my fault just because I wouldn't cry, boohoo, about her school project. I go to Lin's room to see if she wants to go to the market with me but she won't open the door.

• • •

I like to be out in the yard in the morning when it's just getting light. The weeds are wet on my feet and the bottom of my pants but I don't care. I watch for Cat. I leave her some noodles and tofu mixed up on a piece of newspaper. Later when I check, the food's always gone because she's such a hungry cat. I decide to check the alley for any good

78

wood or metal stuff people have thrown out. Even our trash can is piled high today. I wonder why.

It's full of Lin's speed-seed plants. She took such good care of them she even put them in the trash carefully. Speed-seed plants must mean they grow fast. What if I planted them in the old man's yard under the berries, and huge ugly mutant plants spread all over his yard? He'd be out there trying to pull them up or chop them down but they'd just keep growing too fast for him. Lin says they're not mutants, though, because they're all the same. To be a mutant one has to be different but maybe she's wrong and they're not all the same when they get older. I'll just rescue them all and line them up here by the shed. I'll get them all ready so I can plant them in his yard tomorrow.

I go in the kitchen for something to eat. "Du, you're all wet. What are you doing out there?" asks nosy Thuy.

"Nothing," I say. Lin might tell me I can't have her plants even though they were in the trash. Her eyes are still red and she doesn't say anything. She trails off after Thuy and Vuong to school. I see Thuy wait at the bottom of the steps and put her arm around Lin's shoulders. I've got time to plant a few now if I go over the little side-yard fence and hurry. I don't think the old man's up yet.

I like these little plants. They look like they really want to grow. Bigger leaves near the bottom, close together, then smaller ones up the stem, until there are the little tiny growing leaves at the top. They look exactly alike, even more than outside plants do. Even these little tiny, tiny hairs on the stem that I can see if I hold them up to the light.

Wait! Not this one. This one doesn't have any little stem hairs at all. . . . This one doesn't either. I wonder if that's mutant. Little tiny hairs! They're hidden under the leaves and really hard to see. Too bad Lin's already gone to school.

No, I won't just say too bad she's gone. I'll take them to her. It won't take long if I run. I'll be late for school but late just means make up double time in the Counseling Center after school. I don't care about that.

• • •

I can't run too fast with these plants, hairy on the right and no hairs on the left. I don't want to wreck them. The high school's one block down now but there's nobody hanging around out front. Classes must have started.

I find the office by asking a girl in the hall. I park the plants outside the door. I tell the lady inside it's an emergency and give her Lin's name. She doesn't believe me. "I don't know what this is about but you should be in school, young man," she warns me.

"It's my grandma's medicine. She has to have it fast and Lin knows where it is. I'll just ask her and be out of here," I lie. I hope the lie won't come back so my grandma really needs medicine.

"What is your phone number?" she asks.

"We don't have a phone," I lie again.

The lady goes through a file of cards. "There's a phone listed here," she says, like she caught me.

"That's not ours. We got rid of it. Please, lady. Let me just ask her fast." The lady calls the number but nobody answers. My grandma never answers because she can't speak English. Finally that does it. The lady calls a high school girl to take me to Lin's room.

"What are those?" The girl sniffs when she sees the plants in the hall.

"You stay here," she orders me outside a classroom door. She goes inside. She comes out with Lin and jerks her thumb at me. Then she strolls away down the hall.

Lin is scared. "What's wrong with Grandma?" she asks, her red eyes getting teary again.

"Nothing," I answer. I hold out the plants.

"What are you doing with those?" Real tears, angry ones now, roll down her face. "Get out of here!"

"Mutants," I say. "See." I pull her under a window where the light is bright. "See the little hairs." I pull the big leaves at the bottom gently aside so she can see the stem. I'm so excited about it I almost laugh out loud. I show her the other one with no hairs.

"Oh, Du," Lin whispers like I've given her a golden treasure. "I see. I see." Her face goes from golden treasure to disaster again. "Du," she cries. "They're all in the trash. It's trash collection day."

"No, they're not," I say. "They're lined up by the shed."

"Oh, Du. Thank you, thank you. Can you move them inside where they were? Outside might not be good for them. Please, can you do this one last thing? I know you're late for school." I'm afraid she'll cry again.

81

I run home to do what she says. I think about how desperate she is about the stubby plants and their little tiny hairs. Because it's a project for school. I think how cool it is that I found them and saved her. Even though she was so crabby to me before. I get an idea on the way home. Now she can help me just once with Mrs. Dorfman's personal narrative. I'll show my teacher that I had a better trip than anybody if Lin can help me.

• • •

When I walk in, Mrs. Dorfman points toward the office and says "Late slip" to me right in the middle of the social studies paragraph she's reading. I stroll over to the Counseling Center.

"Why are you late, Du?" asks Ms. Whipple. I shrug but I must have a big grin because of rescuing the mutants.

"It's not funny, Du," she says, tilting her head like she's trying to figure something out. "If there's a good reason, you won't have to stay, you know."

"I was rescuing mutants for my sister," I say.

"Okay, Du." She shakes her head while she writes out the late slip but she's smiling a little at what I said. "Be here after school until you make up fifty minutes." I stroll back to class with my late slip. Ms. Whipple's nice. Maybe I will tell her about the mutants.

• • •

82

Lin is so happy to see me when I come home from school late that it's embarrassing. We all look at the plants with the little hairs and the ones without them. "Those are 'glabrous,'" announces Lin. "Most Americans don't even know that word. It means 'smooth, no hairs.'"

"Glabrous," I repeat. "Smooth, no hairs . . . bald." Ha. That old man is glabrous and he doesn't even know it. I'll use it in an essay for Mrs. Dorfman and when she marks it wrong I will tell her what it means.

Thuy and Vuong slap me on the back and tell me how great it is that I saved Lin even though Thuy does say, "What were you going to do with those, anyway?"

"I have to write a personal narrative about a trip I took with my family, and the place we went, and the trip back," I announce. "Will you help me?" They exchange sideways looks. The only place our family goes is Orange and I don't go with them. "I want to tell about going to the Philippines with Grandma," I say, "but I was too little to remember. I know what we did after we got there when I grew older."

"Sure, Du. Sit down here. We'll do it right now." Lin would do almost anything for me now. I wonder if I should waste it on a personal narrative. Then I think about how much she cares about her schoolwork. I'll do a good one once and see what happens.

"Now, about the trip," says Lin, all busy with her paper and pencils ready. "Let's get started."

"Ba and Ma won't tell me anything and Grandma gets sad if I ask and just wants to tell me stories."

"Why do you want to tell that stuff?" asks Thuy. Vuong gets up and leaves the room.

"Because it's my trip!" I'm not going to let them start taking over everything I want to do.

Vuong comes back. "Here," he says, throwing an old newspaper picture on the table. "Here's your trip." We all stare.

In the picture is a little wooden boat pointed at one end and straight at the other. Even without color I can tell the boat is all beaten up and unpainted. It tips a little to one side. The front part is open but the back part has a roof over it. It isn't the boat that's important. There are about forty or fifty Vietnamese people crowded in the front part and on the roof. From the two windows in the side of the boat you can see there are more inside. The people are all staring at whoever is taking the picture, probably on another boat a little way across the water. None of the people are smiling the way Americans do for a picture. They are all skinny and there is a woman with her face hidden under a big hat holding a little boy to keep him from falling off the roof.

I can't believe it. "Is that my boat?" I whisper.

"Nah," answers Vuong. "The newspaper is from 1980 and you went around 1978. But under the picture it says it's a boatload of Vietnamese refugees in the South China Sea. I got it from Nahn up in Orange. He said it's like the one you and Grandma went to the Philippines on. She and Auntie sold their gold bracelets to get a ride. A lot of people drowned or got robbed or killed by pirates but your boat made it."

Vuong knows some other stuff too and he calls Nahn in Orange to find out some more. Thuy and Lin help me write.

I won't let them change what I say too much even though they want to make everything better. Lin wants it perfect but I laugh and say then Mrs. Dorfman will know it's not *my* story. By dinnertime I have a personal narrative with plenty of pages so I draw some little pictures along the edges and a cover because Lin says I should. It's ready to turn in.

My Family Trip
by Du

My family trip was with my grandma and my aunt from Vietnam to the Philippines. Part of my family, which was my dad and mom and my sisters and brother, came to America right away from Vietnam but I was little and had TB and so did my grandma so we went to the Philippines to get better. We stayed there a long time. Then we came to America last summer. We decided to go to the Philippines because there was a war in Vietnam and even after the war there was nothing to eat and no good place to live. My aunt went with us for a while but then she left. My grandma and aunt sold gold jewelry to get a ride on a boat. The boat was very old and tippy and sneaked out at night from the shore so no one would stop us. I don't remember this because I was too little but my uncle told my brother. Everybody got sick because the boat was little and bobbed around so much in the waves. We didn't get attacked by pirates and the boat didn't tip over so we made it. It took a long time. I don't remember where we stayed when we first got to the Philippines but they had special camps for people from Vietnam.

Our camp wasn't like a camp in America. I got older there because we were there about eight years while we waited. We lived in different houses. The houses there were not in rows with streets and sidewalks like houses here. Some had concrete floors but most were very little and parts of them were made out of thatch from the kind of trees they have there. Sometimes we lived with other people my grandma knew and sometimes just us. Sometimes the wind blew very hard and long and there was dust in the air and sometimes it rained a long time and got muddy. There was a well near the houses and in some places faucets not far away. A lot of airplanes flew over the camp.

We waited in lines for long hours in the hot sun to get bags of rice and beans and sometimes sugar. When I was older I figured out how to squeeze into the lines when people looked the other way. If they yelled at me I just ducked away further up the line. I learned where to get mangoes and bananas too because we liked them. I got the food so my grandma didn't have to stand and wait in line. When my grandma felt good we sold food she made. Our store was a blanket near the road. Her food sold fast. She made spring rolls and little golden round buns. She burned pieces of thatch and wood I collected for her in our little black stove so she could cook. I collected the money. Other people sold noodles and jewelry and other stuff. If we made enough money I went to school. There we all sat squished up on benches to learn English and math and history. We all talked Vietnamese. The best time was when we didn't have enough money for school. Me and my friends would run down to the ocean or around the edges of the camp or play cards or marbles or have cricket fights if it was raining. I would catch great big shiny beetles and tie them on a string and follow them when they flew. If we found a dead bird we made feather birdies and kicked them around a circle with our feet. I never missed. I would like to go back to my friends there and run along the ocean right now. I would give away the rolls we sold so I would never have to sit on the school benches. I'd be outside almost all day.

When we got over having TB we still had to wait to come to America. My dad sent money so we could buy plane tickets and come to live with him and my mom and my sisters and brother. We flew in an airplane that took days and nights to get here because the Philippines are on the other side of the world and also we waited a long time in airports.

The End

● ● ●

I have my personal narrative in my notebook. If I turned it in now it would be late but Mrs. Dorfman just collected

Tiffany's and Jorge's. "Better late than never," she said. "I'll take ten points off your final score for each late day."

She asks for volunteers to read theirs. Alan volunteers to read about his trip to Carlsbad Beach in an RV. Then Emily reads about some place but she talks so soft and it's so boring that I don't listen. After Anthony reads his, Mrs. Dorfman says, "I'd like to speak to you after class, Anthony."

"How come?" he blurts. "I did it."

"Are you sure you didn't get quite a bit of help?" she asks with her eyebrows up. Anthony mutters about how she blames him for everything, and slumps down in his seat. Veronica's trip to Mexico takes less than a minute to read. Kids are squirming around like me and nobody's listening. Mrs. Dorfman's grading our spelling tests. She handed back my Disneyland paper with the others but I don't volunteer. I almost raise my hand to read my real personal narrative but then I start to think about it. Maybe they won't believe it about the pirates and the boat and the jewelry. Mrs. Dorfman might not like the part about cutting in line and Anthony will laugh and say we were "trash pickers." It's not really what Mrs. Dorfman said we should write anyway because it took years and years, not a week or a few days. And also it's late so it won't get a good grade anyway. I don't want a D on this paper. She'll say I didn't write it because Thuy and Lin helped me. And then I think that I just don't want her or any of them to read it or hear it now. It's mine. I just found out myself about the boat. Vuong said hundreds of thousands of people died in those boats. I'll just keep it for myself and maybe someday if I have American kids I'll let them read it.

The Bicycle

I can get through that little window so fast now the old man couldn't see me if he could see around corners. He's got boxes of Christmas junk in this trunk. Strings of lights and colored balls. Some of them are broken but I didn't break them. Maybe that boy in the picture album did. I bet that's his box of metal parts way down in the bottom of the trunk. I wonder what he made with it. I could make almost anything out of this stuff. These little gears and rods fit right onto the wheels. I wish I had one of these sets but I never even saw one in a store. It's very old. It would cost a lot new.

That boy in the picture must be the old man's son. He must have played stupid baseball all the time. He's got on baseball clothes in almost every picture. The lady must be his mother. She smiles nice. I wonder what happened to them. I never saw anyone come to see that mean old man. I guess that's why he spies on us all the time. I still owe him back for when he stank up my shoes and called the police about the blackberries. I gotta think of something good. The lawn mower doesn't count because he put it back together right in front of our window.

● ● ●

Maybe I shouldn't have left the little machine I made in the shed. It's too good to take apart. I don't think that old man will find it. Now I've got nothing to do. "Do your homework." That's what they'll say if I go inside. It's trash collection day. The alley's got a lot of junk in it. I'll find something for my catapult.

A bike! A real kid's bike sticking out from under this smelly old mattress. Somebody crashed it but I can fix it. I'll straighten the wheels and handlebars. The seat's missing so I'll make one. It was a good bike before it got crashed. The back tire's still good. I got a lot of work in front of me and I don't want anyone to see. They might not let me keep it.

● ● ●

The bike's almost finished. I'll melt this old rubber piece to fix the tire. My cat likes to watch me. Burning this rubber stuff makes my nose hurt and my eyes water.

Who's yelling? "Du, Du! . . ."

"What in tarnation's goin' on . . . ?"

People are yelling all at once like someone's being murdered. Thuy's yelling from our house and the old man's on his back porch yelling. Vietnamese and English all yelled together. I can't understand either one of them.

I better go see what it is. Ow! Something bites my leg. The grass is on fire! I'm gonna be in trouble. Jump up and down on the grass. Ow! Bare feet aren't good for this. But I have tough feet. It's almost out.

It was only a little fire. What are they so excited about? Thuy and the old man are both yelling again. They go back inside. They slam the doors. I look at my cat. She's still sitting, watching. She knows I wouldn't let everything burn up. I'll get her something to eat.

"You love it best when I bring fish, don't you, Cat?" Thuy didn't know I was working on a bike. She thought I was just burning up the grass. Why would I do that? "Here, Cat. Here's an extra piece of fish I saved. You don't have to lick the paper. That's right. Come and get it. I won't hurt you. . . . Oh yeah, run away now that you've got the fish. See, Cat. You're my pet. You took it right out of my hand and nothing bad happened. See you later."

● ● ●

Wow! This bike doesn't go straight but it goes pretty fast. I've got a bike! I'll ride it to school. I'll do wheelies. Air goes out of the tires pretty fast but I can put more air in. Who would leave a bike like this just lying in the alley? Wait till Thuy and Lin and Vuong find out I've got a bike. They never had one. They probably don't even know how to ride one. I only fell over a few times at first. They wouldn't know how to fix the tires and straighten out the handlebars. I wonder if my dad will let me keep it. I'll hide it for a while until I find a seat. He'll say a seat will cost money. I don't need to sit down to ride anyway. To go fast you stand up on the pedals.

Here comes that old man home from the store. He's staring at me, spying as usual. I'll show him how fast I can go. I'll jump this curb. That old man walks so slow he'd never catch me on this bike. I could go skidding all around him and he'd never lay a finger on me. I ride up behind him on the sidewalk very quiet and go by him so fast he jumps. I'm going to ride all day until dark. I'll just go tell my grandma where I am so she doesn't worry.

● ● ●

"Du, where'd you get a bike? You give it to me right now!" My dad shouts at me from the porch. I rode too long and he saw me.

I'm so surprised I don't have time to think. I don't lie to my dad. I'd never lie. "I just borrowed it to ride for a little while. From someone down the alley." As soon as I say it I know it is wrong. I found it in the alley and I hid it in the alley again but I didn't really borrow it in the alley. Maybe if I just leave it hidden there and don't ride it, it won't matter if I lied. How does my dad know I have a bike? I stayed away from the front of the house but they must have seen me anyway.

"And don't you go bothering that man next door again. He said you almost ran him over. We don't want any trouble with the neighbors. If I hear of any more . . ."

So the old man came over and told my dad about the bike and complained just because I rode by him fast. I wish he'd leave me alone. I hope no one finds the bike in that junky place between the garages. I won't ride it anymore, I guess, but I'll just keep it there for a while.

Free Orange

I wish I could ride my bike. I went to visit it for just a minute and it was still there. It's a great bike after I fixed it but now I can't ride it. I'm lucky about one thing, though. Just when I need a bicycle seat I find one in the trash. Just sticking up there like it wants me to find it. It's the old banana-shaped kind that guys don't use anymore but it fit right on the seat post. I rode one circle around the alley with the seat on and then I had to hide it again. I won't ride it.

That's the front gate slamming. I wonder who it is.

It's only Lin but she's talking to somebody. She's talking to that old man across the fence.

"What are you talking to him about?" I meet her at the door.

"About you, little Du," she teases, pushing past me.

"Tell me!" I'm mad. I don't want him to know stuff about me. I'm mad because he told my dad about the bike and now I can't ride it and it's mine. I fixed it. I follow Lin into the dining room.

"He just wants to know if you're my brother," she answers, opening her backpack. "I said no," she adds, laughing. Thuy and Vuong laugh too.

"I am your brother," I yell. Lin laughs more. That old man doesn't know about what happened. He doesn't know about the boats that left Vietnam in the dark and if you weren't on them you never got another chance to get out. My mom and dad had to leave me because I was just a baby and my grandma and I had TB. We waited and waited to get medicine and for her to get better. You can't come if you have TB. They wanted to get us here but they couldn't for a long time. Lots of people don't know that here. On TV the families live together forever in big houses.

I can see that nosy old man out in front. He's looking proud at his big orange tree. Big oranges so ripe they're getting wrinkled but he won't let anybody eat them. There's no way he can eat them all by himself but he keeps them all anyway.

I've got an idea. If I can't ride my bike he's not going to eat his oranges. I have to find some cardboard in the alley.

• • •

Here, Cat. Your dinner's mostly soy milk and rice but there's a little piece of chicken I saved too. Eat it up. You can watch me while I paint these signs. I had to borrow one of Thuy's black smelly markers to make good big signs. "Neatness makes people want to read what you have to say," says Mrs. Dorfman. I'm not usually neat but I will be now. See. You're a fat cat lately, Cat. Maybe I better bring you a diet soda like Americans drink.

I wish that old man would go someplace. I can't put up the signs unless he's gone. He doesn't have any friends to visit or to eat his oranges because he's so mean. I saw those pictures of his son and his wife. Maybe his wife is dead. He's old. But his son doesn't visit him either.

• • •

Finally that old man is leaving. He's walking to the bus stop with those skinny white legs sticking out of those shorts. Now for his orange tree. I'll put up those signs and he'll get a big surprise when he gets back. I have to be quick and do it when no one is looking. He'll never know it was me. Lots of people like the look of those oranges. Maybe I wish he did know it was me. He has to know he can't spy and wreck my shirt and smell up my shoes and take away my bike and get away with it. He never knew I messed up his lawn mower. At least, he never told my dad. I don't want to do anything to the stuff in his shed now. Cat sleeps there and I don't want him to find her. He might hurt her. And I like to make stuff with that building set in the trunk. I don't want him to figure that out and lock it up. This'll be good enough if it works. It has to work. I'll just put this one sign up fast on his fence right in front of the tree. Now run down the street and put the other one at the busy corner. He'll see it when he comes home but it'll be too late.

It's fun waiting for the bus in front of my sign. FREE ORANGE in big black letters with an arrow. It looks great. Lots of people saw it. Some of them are still down there picking oranges. I didn't pick any so it's not my fault if they're all gone. Here comes the Number 10. That's the one he took.

He's creaking down the bus stairs. He sees the sign but he doesn't get it. He's got grocery bags to carry. He's getting closer. He can see his orange tree if he looks up. There! He sees it. He's starting to run but it's a pretty slow little run. That Mexican lady's getting in her car with a box of oranges. "Gracias," she calls. He drops his groceries down to go faster.

He's at his fence but it's too late. All but the very top oranges are gone. He doesn't even tear up the sign. He just creaks up the stairs into his house like he's sad and he doesn't even see that guy in the tree that waves at him. Now we're even. I paid him back for what he did to me. I'm laughing. Kind of. I wonder what my grandma would say if she knew.

The Thief

I got a bike now like all the other guys in my class but I can't ride it. I wonder what would happen if I rode it just once to show them. Even this morning no one would see me. My grandma's asleep and everybody else is gone. I could go down the alley and hide it again after school. Later I'll tell my dad how I didn't really borrow it, I *found* it in the alley because someone threw it away and I fixed it up.

• • •

I hate school. I ride my bike to school for the first time and the principal is out at the bike rack. He hurries over when he sees me. "You have to lock your bike up to leave it here, Du," he tells me.

"Not that thing," says Anthony, behind the principal's back. "Who'd want it?" I look mean at Anthony so he knows I won't forget he said that.

"You have to take it home unless you lock it." The principal says it again louder. A teacher hurries over to talk to him.

"The seat looks like a piece of doo-doo, Du Du," whispers Jorge. "The tires are flat. Did it cost a dime or a nickel?" I want to make Jorge shut up but I don't know what to do with my bike. I feel dumb just standing there.

"You can lock it up with mine." It's Todd, who sits in the front of the room so I don't talk to him much. He puts his chain through both our bikes. I walk off to class with him and leave the principal and Anthony and Jorge behind.

● ● ●

I stop to visit my bike on my way to the dumbest reading group in Room 10. It looks cool lined up in the bike rack with all the others and it's mine. I don't care if I'm late to Room 10 because we're reading the story about a skinny girl in a covered wagon for the third time. Some kids in the group still can't read it. We have to answer when the teacher shows us the cards with the hard words on them. They're so easy I won't answer. I have to sit there while

Jennifer reads out loud. It takes her fifteen minutes to read a page. I think about my bike. I think I'll look for a board so I can make a ramp to jump off.

● ● ●

I visit my bike again on the way back to Mrs. Dorfman's. Everybody's talking at once when I get back to class but I can't figure out what's happening. Mrs. Dorfman doesn't even mind when everybody blurts. She never likes it when I blurt, which is one of the reasons I don't say anything anymore. I feel dumb raising my hand like the kids in front.

We all go to recess. Anthony and Jorge get me out in four square by teaming up. Anthony hits it real soft and high to Jorge and Jorge slams it out of reach in the corner of my square. I go mess around at the gym bars. I stroll in slowly when the bell rings.

Veronica's got her hand raised, waving it around like she's trying to chase flies. "Boys and girls, please get out your math papers from yesterday," Mrs. Dorfman says. She won't look at Veronica. Veronica won't put her hand down. Mrs. Dorfman finally says, "Veronica," in a tired voice. Everyone knows she's going to complain about something from recess.

"Du stole my brother's bike," she says. "I saw it locked up in the bike rack and Christie said it's Du's. He rode it to school. He stole it from my brother a month ago."

"I did not!" I blurt.

"If there's stolen property, it's a matter for the police," announces Mrs. Dorfman. "I am not paid enough to be judge and jury for everything that goes on around here. Veronica, after math you may go and discuss this with Mr. Martin." We correct our math papers. Mine doesn't need correcting but I see that Veronica's does. A lot. When she gets up to sharpen her pencil my foot is out in the aisle. She's so clumsy she trips right over it. No one would care except she hits her big mouth on the corner of Tiffany's desk and her lip starts to bleed. It's just a little bit of blood. Nobody at this school cares what anyone says to you or what they do to you but if there's even a little bit of blood the teacher acts like you murdered somebody.

"He tripped me," cries Veronica, struggling to her feet.

"I did not," I blurt. "She tripped herself."

"He stuck his foot out. I saw it," calls out Rosaria. She's Veronica's friend.

Mrs. Dorfman is angrily scribbling on a yellow slip for the Counseling Center. Good, I think. I won't have to sit here for boring math.

The Counseling Center is the same as always. I look at magazines. Ms. Whipple talks to me about kindness to others. I nod and say, "Uh-huh." The phone rings. Suddenly it's different. The principal wants to see me this time. I sit on a hard chair outside his office. I watch the secretary work the computer for an hour. She never looks at me. The principal calls me into his office.

"What do your parents think of this type of behavior, Du?" he says. I shrug. "That's what I thought." I make myself look at his face like Vuong said I should. His eyebrows go right across his nose. "Report back here after school," he commands, pointing to the door. He tips his head back and both eyebrows raise up. I go so I don't have to look anymore.

• • •

I sit at the table in his office. I hear everybody laughing and messing around outside as they go home. His table has piles of papers on it and a bowl like a frog with paper-wrapped candy and crumbs in it. He doesn't offer me any. I don't want it anyway. I copy the school rules over and over on cheap paper that tears if I erase. But I don't have to erase. It's not hard. I can do it without even thinking. Sometimes instead of "I will respect the rights and property of others" I write "I will respect the fights and potato chips of others." Nobody's going to read them. I don't know how long I'm supposed to do it but I never look up and I never ask.

It's like sewing. I don't think about anything anymore. I just do it. One page, both sides. Two pages. Three. Four. The principal shuts off his computer and stands up. I keep writing. "I hope you have learned your lesson, Du." He holds out his hand for my stack of papers. I don't want to look at his face but I hand them to him. He tears up all my copying and throws it in the trash. "You may go home," he says. "Your parents have been notified about the stolen property." I leave. He called my dad at work again. He told him about my bike. He doesn't know that now my eyes are hot and my insides feel tight. He has won.

Todd's gone but my bike's in the rack. I should ditch it in the alley on the way home. But it's my bike. I fixed it. It goes pretty fast after I pump up the tires. And I didn't steal it. I found it. I'll just ride it home and tell my dad even if he is mad. He'll know I rode it to school anyway.

I felt angry when Veronica said I stole her brother's bike but now I don't feel angry. I know it's going to turn into a big thing. I want to just keep riding my bike straight down the street to wherever the street ends. Someplace out where there are just trees and grass. Except my front tire's getting flat.

I cross Fortieth Street. At the end of my street a car screeches up next to me and a bunch of big Mexican guys jump out.

"There's the kid," they yell.

"You messed up my sister, *muchacho*. You're gonna pay."

"You stole my bike, you little runt. And you wrecked it too."

I ride around a tree that blocks them for a second while I get past. I take off down the street on my bike; two of them run after me. The other two pile back in the car and come screeching along behind.

Tire, don't go flat now. I'm almost home. I hate being scared. I hate them.

I slam in the gate. At the same time my dad slams out onto the steps from inside the house. I know the only reason he's home now is because he got the call from the principal. The Mexican guys chasing me stop for a second at our fence. They yell angry stuff at us in Mexican. I hang on tight to my bike. If I leave it to run inside they might take it. Then one, two of them push through our gate. My dad is down the steps like a tiger. I drop the bike behind me to stand with him if they try to do anything to him and he needs help. There is a flurry. Mostly grabbing shirts and pushing. I get knocked down but I am up again fast.

Sirens! A screech of brakes. The Mexican guys and my dad and me stand facing each other across the little broken walk that goes up to our front door. Angry ugly scary faces. Rough breathing. Two policemen run up with their clubs out. They push between us on the little walk. One makes the Mexicans step back. The other moves toward my father and me.

"Get off my property! Don't touch my son!" He stands where he is. Mexican and Vietnamese and English words fill the air. One of the Mexican guys lunges at my bike. For a moment I pull and he pulls. The policeman with a red mustache makes him let go.

"He stole the bike. He beat up our sister," the guy yells. He is young but with thick muscles and short dark bristly hair. He is so angry he is like a wire about to snap. The policeman herds him over to a corner of the yard.

The other policeman, a big black guy like a football guy on TV, talks to me. "You steal that bike?" he asks. He looks at the bike with a snort like it's not worth stealing.

"No," I yell like the Mexican guy so they'll believe me. "I found it."

"Why you hide it from everybody, then?" my dad shouts. "Why do you say you borrow it?" What he says helps the Mexican guys. He thinks I stole it too.

"Well?" asks the policeman quietly because he's sure I stole it.

How can I tell them all the stuff so they'll listen? How can I tell them that I found it under a mattress in the alley and fixed it and it didn't have a seat and now it does because I found a seat too and I didn't tell them because I didn't want them to make me get rid of it because we don't have bikes and it just seemed like a good thing to hide it for a while. It's too much to say. They won't listen to it all. The truth is simple. I don't say anything except, "I found it," with my head down. I know they won't believe me. A great bike like this just lying around someplace.

The red mustache policeman comes back from the squad car. "It doesn't belong to either one of them," he announces. "A bike with that number was reported missing up in North County a couple of months ago. You can all go home now." He crosses his arms and stares at the Mexican guys.

"What about he beat up our sister?" yells the bristly-haired guy from the corner of the yard.

"That's another matter. You'll have to file a complaint," says the black policeman, sighing.

My dad looks like he's gonna jump on me now. "She tripped at school," I say, looking down. I know he won't believe this either.

The policemen wait until the Mexican guys get in their car and roar away. They put my bike in the squad car. They finish writing down some stuff. The red mustache one looks at me where I stand behind my dad. "Where do you think you're gonna end up if you steal stuff?" he asks. I shrug. My dad swats at me. "You listen to your dad, young man," the policeman says. His radio blares and he and the black policeman walk to their car and drive slowly away. I see people who live near us outside their houses, staring. Of course that old man is outside too. He's almost falling over his fence, he's trying so hard to hear.

My dad grabs the back of my shirt. I twist and see his angry face. Behind him Thuy and Lin and Vuong stare out from the front door. Nobody will believe me. I duck down and yank away. My dad would never expect me to do that. He loses his grip on my shirt. I run. He shouts. I run faster away to the backyard. I jump the back fence. I run down the alley toward the big apartments at the end of our block.

I sit around outside the wall there until I'm so cold and hungry that's all I can think about. I don't want to go home but I don't know where else to go. Finally I think of the shed. I go back down the alley. I climb through the window into the shed. It's pretty dark in there now with the last daylight from the window. Cat is curled up asleep in the corner on some old bags. Her slit eyes partly open when she hears me come in. I sit on the trunk for a while. I don't want to make anything out of the building set now. Slowly I crawl over to Cat. I talk to her in Vietnamese. She watches me carefully but she stays curled up there. I stick out my hand. She sniffs my fingers. I don't have any food but she lets me pet her smooth warm fur. She purrs.

My stomach hurts. I am so hungry. I want something to eat so bad I'm thinking about going into the house. I don't care what my dad does. Maybe he's not so mad now or he's gone back to work. He doesn't believe me about the bike. He'd believe the others but they'd never fix up a cool bike.

Now it's gone. At least those Mexican guys didn't get it. Stupid Veronica went home and told about the bike and said I beat her up. The principal made me write all those lines and then called my dad anyway.

I talk to Cat because she trusts me. "Cat, you're the only one that believes me. I came in here and you're all curled up and warm and you let me pet you when I don't even have any food. I'll bring you something later. I'll have to hurry so I'll just throw it through the window. Watch for it." I say good-bye to Cat. I climb through the window again. I take a deep breath and walk up the back stairs. I hope my dad went back to work.

It is quiet when I open the back door. I know I have to face them. I walk into the dining room. Thuy and Lin and Vuong look up from their books. They jump up from their chairs. Everybody yells at once. My dad is still home. He and my mom crowd around the table with the others. Everybody shouts how bad I am. Except my grandma. She just looks so sad as she takes my arm and sits me at the table. I don't want to cry. My mom is crying. My dad is tight and angry, waiting for the others to finish their yelling.

He makes a big circle with his arm. It means "Get out of here." The others know what it means. They shuffle out. Even my grandma. I wait with my head down.

He stands over me. "We did not come here to be robbers," he growls. "You bring shame to the whole family."

I wait. "I didn't steal it," I choke. "I found it." He doesn't say anything. I think he wants to believe it but he can't. He doesn't know what to do. Nobody in our family ever stole before.

He shouts in Vietnamese. "Stealing? Robbing people of what they work for? Beating girls at school? This is shameful. Dishonor for our whole family like . . ." I am sitting frozen here at the table afraid to move because he might explode. The doorbell rings. No one ever rings our doorbell late at night. More trouble. It is the police or even the Mexicans returning. My dad stops yelling to listen.

A man's voice talks English from the front doorway. My dad strides out to see who it is. I creep across the room to hear too.

"Madam, I couldn't help overhearing the incident on the sidewalk today." It's the voice of the old spy next door. I stick my head around the door to the living room. He's standing in our doorway with his bald head and his bushy eyebrows. He's talking to my mom, who opened the door. Thuy and Lin and Vuong are behind her. Nobody says anything. My mom probably doesn't understand what he's talking about. The old man changes his voice. He talks very loud and slow. "Your boy did not steal that bike," he announces. "I saw it in the alley, piled on the garbage cans, the night before he found it. I am the one who threw away the bicycle seat." There's silence. "Well," he says. "Just thought you'd want to know." He turns to shuffle back down the stairs.

"Wait, wait," my mom cries, grabbing the back of his sweater. He stops. She pushes past the others to run to the kitchen. She comes back with a plate covered with a paper towel. "For you, for you," she says. "Thank you. Thank you." She bows. She hands him the plate. I think she's crying again.

He takes the plate. "Thank you, madam," he says. He goes home.

Now they're all talking at once again. They're laughing. My mom's laughing and crying. Only my dad's not laughing. "So, not a robber," he says, "but still lying, hitting girls at your school." He shakes his head sadly like that's something beyond understanding. I start to explain but he interrupts. "You lied about the bike, borrowed it, you said." He turns his back on me and walks slowly to his room. My grandma hurries to the stove to make some food. The plate my mom gave to the old man was the dinner my grandma saved for me. Golden spring rolls with a bowl of red sauce. Now I'll have soup with noodles.

I lie on the couch at night when everybody has gone to bed. The old man came over to tell my family the truth. Even after I played that mean trick with his oranges. I wonder why. He threw that old bicycle seat away for me to find. I feel bad about his oranges. I guess I won't trick him anymore. I wonder if the Mexican guys will try to get me when the police aren't around. They still think I stole the bike. So does everybody at school. The Mexican guys think I beat up Veronica too.

Headless

Thuy slams the front door. She races to Lin and Vuong, studying at the table. She's yelling and jumping around. Thuy never slams the door and she never yells and jumps. This could be interesting. I leave the TV. I check the window but I don't see the old man watching.

"I won! I won!" Thuy cries, waving around a piece of paper. We crowd near her as she brushes papers aside and puts the paper in the middle of the empty space. A little piece of paper. "Thuy Nguyen," it says on one line. At the end of the line it says "$250.00."

"A check for two hundred and fifty dollars. Wow!" Vuong is impressed.

"My poster!" Thuy cries. "My Fair Housing poster won first prize."

I remember the thing. She was crabby when I drank orange juice near her while she was working on it. "Get out of here, Du. Don't spill that," she ordered. She had her nose down to that poster for days, coloring little tiny houses all over it. She covered the table with eraser crumbs until late at night. Still, I wish I had that much money. She'll give it to my dad, of course.

• • •

Saturday is a long day. I get up early to look for Cat. I blow some weed seeds toward the old man's grass. He was okay about the bike. The seeds won't grow anyway or he'll pull them up before they have a chance. He'll get some exercise. It's good for him. I watch cartoons.

Thuy calls from her bedroom. "Get ready, Du. We're going to Fashion Valley."

"I don't want to go," I say. I don't know what Fashion Valley is but if Thuy likes it, it's boring.

"Okay," Thuy says. Thuy and Lin and Vuong head for the door. Now I might want to go.

"All right. I'll come," I say like I don't really want to. I don't know if I do or not.

"Your shirt's dirty. Get your jacket," orders Lin. It's going to be like this all day, I think, but I follow them out the door.

We wait at the bus stop. Thuy has a hundred dollars. She gave her prize money to my dad but he gave some of it back. He's proud of her for winning over all the other kids. He thinks you should get paid for work.

Thuy pays for us on the bus. We bounce along. More and more people get on the bus. Vuong gives his seat to an old lady. He jerks me out of my seat by my arm so another lady gets my seat. She's not so old. I think of my grandma. I'd want people to let her sit down. The bus sways around a corner. It's fun trying to hold on. We stop. Everybody's pushing to get off.

Huge stores with sidewalks as wide as three houses, and more big sidewalks above them. Fancy lights and glass everywhere. Music. Crowds of people. Good smells. This is Fashion Valley. We go in a big store. It's where Americans buy all the fancy stuff I see on TV.

Thuy hurries us into a store that sells cameras. In the back is a big cardboard thing that has snowy hills and pine trees painted on it. Thuy has a coupon from the paper. She makes us all get in front of the snow things to get our picture taken. I feel dumb. The guy who takes the pictures pushes us around to the right place. I'm in front. "Cheese," he says. I wrinkle up my nose. I hate cheese. His camera flashes.

Thuy chooses a frame for the picture. She pays. They'll send it to my mom and dad when it's ready. "It's a Christmas picture," I complain. "Christmas isn't for a long time." Also Thuy knows we don't do Christmas.

"Ho ho ho, Merry Christmas," shouts Vuong, pretending

to be dumb Santa Claus. Lin swats him. Thuy hurries us out of the store.

Some people are dressed funny because today is Halloween. I know about Halloween from school. "NO COSTUMES AT SCHOOL" said the paper we took home. Kids were excited but I didn't listen much because our family doesn't do Halloween either. Here, people that look old enough to be moms and dads are running around with skeleton stuff on and one lady is dressed like a football player. I'm looking at her and I walk into a witch. She gives me a mean look. Pumpkin stuff's around too. I'd like to make a pumpkin face with a knife.

One store has a window full of Halloween stuff. There's a rubber mask with blood running down the face and the eyeballs falling out. I could put that on when the old man spies in our window. He'd probably fall over. I try it on. Thuy laughs. "You look much better," says Lin. Now Vuong laughs. Thuy shows me how much the mask costs. Way too much. She buys me a tube of fake blood and an eyeball to glue on with red rubber strings. I'll make a mask.

"We're going to see *Hidden Planet* but it's too early. We'll go shopping," announces Thuy. I don't know what *Hidden Planet* is but Thuy has the money so we all go where she wants. She looks at clothes in a big store that smells like very sweet flowers and has a guy playing an extra-big shiny piano. "Escalator," says Thuy, pointing at the moving stairs and nodding at me like I'm dumb. I know *escalator* from TV. I've seen them a lot. But it's fun to ride. Thuy and Lin try on clothes, and Vuong and me ride the escalator. The security guard won't let you go down the one that's going up.

Vuong and me go to a store that sells good knives and magnets and thermometers and sets of wooden balls you hit with a club. I wish I could buy one.

"Cody. Hey, Cody," someone yells. Vuong turns around. Two guys walk up to us and slap Vuong's hand.

"What's goin' on?"

"How ya doin?" They talk fast to Vuong about stuff. I'm not sure what they're talking about.

"What's Cody?" I ask when they leave.

"It's my school name. Don't tell, okay?" answers Vuong.

"Okay," I say. I think about it. Kids make fun of *Du* but it's my name. I wouldn't change it. What good is it anyway if you change your name and don't tell anyone?

"We got a phone call for Cody from a beautiful girl but I didn't know who Cody was so I hung up," I tell him.

"How could you tell she was beautiful over the phone?" he says, sneering. I know he has girls' names inside his notebook. I looked.

"I could tell," I say.

"Really?" he asks. "Now you know. I'm Cody. Give me the phone next time."

"Okay, Cody, my man," I say like his friends. He starts chasing me through the crowds.

Vuong and me wonder if it's time for *Hidden Planet*. We find Thuy and Lin. Thuy is standing in front of a mirror in the store. She has on a red leather jacket. Thuy takes off her glasses. She turns in front of the mirror. She smiles at herself like when she won the poster contest.

"Wow! That's beautiful!" breathes Lin. It looks like a jacket that is too small to me.

I grab the price tag. "It's almost a hundred dollars," I say, laughing. No way Thuy's going to have that. She hangs it up carefully. We follow her to the movie. She's very bossy about how I walk through the store. "Don't touch things," she snaps at me. She looks embarrassed when I touch a coat with a fur collar anyway. It's softer than Cat. She bumps into me on purpose. I know she doesn't want me here. I watch her walking ahead of me looking at all the fancy things. When I get some money someday I'll buy her the red jacket.

We wait in line at the movie. Thuy pays. We go in with a whole bunch of other people, mostly kids. Right inside the door is another long line of people waiting to buy food. I'm hungry. Food smells everywhere make me hungrier. Candy piled higher than the top of my head in back against a mirror. Drinks coming out of hoses. A glass box with popcorn piled inside. Popcorn smell makes my mouth water. Thuy hurries us by the food.

We sit in front in the movie. I have to tip my head back to see. It's very loud. The movie is about a spaceship that gets sucked into a hole and crashes near an ocean. They try to find people there because there are some empty buildings. I'm not sure what's going on but people laugh a lot. I'm very hungry. Food smells followed us into the theater. Everybody around us has food. A long talking part comes near the end of the movie. "I'm hungry," I finally whisper to Thuy.

She pushes some money into my hand. "Bring back the change," she whispers. I go to the food place. I see she gave me ten dollars. I'll buy something for all of us. No one's in line now but me.

"Four drinks," I tell the girl, who looks about as old as Thuy.

"What kind?" she asks like I'm dumb.

I look at the machine. "Pepsi, of course," I answer like she's the dumb one. "And popcorn and a box of those." I point at one of the big boxes of candy. They don't have any small boxes. Me and Thuy and Lin and Vuong are gonna have a feast in there.

The girl brings four drinks. Each one is big enough for four people. She tosses down the box of candy. "Popcorn'll be ready in a minute," she says. She walks away. The drinks are too full to carry without spilling. I drink a little from each one. I open the candy. "Raisinettes," it says on the box. I eat some. They're sweet but good. Raisins covered with chocolate.

The girl comes back with my popcorn. It's in a huge round tub. I wonder how I can carry it all. "Twenty-four sixty," she says.

Uh-oh. "This is all I got," I say, throwing the ten-dollar bill on the counter.

She grabs back the popcorn. "You drank outa those. You opened the candy. I'm callin' the manager. You stay right there." I want to run but Thuy and Lin and Vuong are inside and I don't know where to go.

The manager comes out from a place under the stairs

116

when the girl calls on the phone. He hurries over. I don't look at his face. "You go with him while he locates his parents," he orders the girl.

The stupid girl follows me to Thuy and Lin and Vuong. People hiss at us to be quiet while she talks to them. We all go out to the manager. Thuy has to pay for the drinks and the raisins. I don't even want them anymore. Thuy doesn't want to go back in the movie.

Outside the movie Thuy and Lin and Vuong all yell at me at once.

"You're stupid, Du. Why did you have to be such a pig?"

"Can't you add?"

"There's no prices!" I tell Vuong. He points inside high over the mirror. All the prices are written there. I never saw them. Vuong turns away with disgust.

"You ruined the whole day," Thuy chokes. "Now I don't have enough money left for the bus. How are we gonna get home?" They won't stop. They keep yelling at me. Thuy looks like she's going to cry. I ruined her special day.

I don't want to be yelled at anymore. I push my bag with the blood and eyeball into Thuy's hands. "Take it back for bus money," I yell back at them as I run. "I'll see you at home." They shout and run after me but they can never catch me. I hide in a store and watch them running around outside.

"Can I help you?" says a lady who doesn't sound like she wants to help me at all. I escape through the side door of the store. I think I know how to get home. We passed over the freeway in the bus and I know it goes under Fortieth Street not too far from our house. It's a long way. All I had was four sips of Pepsi and some raisins. Better get started. I trot along the streets filled with cars.

I wish Vuong didn't say I was stupid. I wasn't so stupid. The sign with the prices was too high. I bet Thuy and Lin and Vuong are still looking for me. They'll ride the bus home and look out the windows. I'll take a shortcut. I won't get lost if I keep going in the right direction. I know about where our house is. I have to go up to the top of the big hill and over about ten blocks.

There's no place to walk on this bridge. I'll cut under. Hey! There's water here. Not much water. Just a lot of tall weeds around big, deep puddles but there's some ducks even. If it rains it'll be a real river. I didn't know they had this stuff here except on TV. I bet I could catch frogs. Even fish. My grandma says the Mekong River in Vietnam is huge, too far to see across in some places. But this one is a nice little river. I'll remember. I'll come back and catch a fish for Cat. All the people driving by on the bridge don't even know it's here. It'll be my secret river.

Now I'm on the other side, I'm not so sure where I am. I'll figure it out. It's getting dark but up ahead are streets with houses. Those must be Halloween kids. One kid's a ghost and another's a dancer or something. I'd be a *mea heo*. It's a pig ghost in Vietnam. My grandma says it tangles up your legs if you go walking out at night.

A lot of kids are out here. I'm hungry. I wonder what would happen if I just went with them to the door. They're too little to catch me if I run and their moms have babies in carts.

"Trick or treat!"

118

"Happy Halloween." The lady who answers the door is big and smiling. She puts candy in the kids' bags. "Oooh," she says. "A ghost. A princess." She sees me. "What are you?" she asks. I shrug. She hands me a Tootsie Roll.

"Thank you. Happy Halloween," the American kids call behind them. Their moms give me funny looks. They walk close behind the kids so I can't follow them. I don't need to.

I go up to a door. I ring and ring the doorbell. No one answers. I knock. No one answers. I eat my Tootsie Roll. I go next door. A light is on and a pumpkin is in the window. I ring the bell. A man answers. "What are you?" he asks. I get mad. Then I remember he means what am I dressed like for Halloween. I shrug. "Get a costume and come back, kid," he says. He shuts the door. I stand outside. If I don't get a treat do I get to do a trick? I ring the bell again. I zip my jacket up fast over my head so it looks like my head got cut off. I hear the door open. "Trick or treat," I yell through my jacket. I wait. "Where's your bag?" he asks. I shrug but it's hard because my jacket is tight over my head. I hold out my hand. I wait. I hear him walk away and come back. "Here," he says, pushing something stringy into my hand. I think he's laughing. I don't want to get tricked. "Happy Halloween," he says. I hear the door shut. I unzip my jacket. I got a grocery bag with handles and a big chocolate bar inside. This is fun.

I go to all the houses. If they're dark they don't answer so I quit going to those. I don't want to waste my time. I get a bunch of candy and an apple. I eat the apple. It's good. At every door I zip my jacket over my head. I can't see them and they can't see me but they give me candy.

There's a smashed pumpkin in the middle of the street. It's not very big. It's cracked in two. I bet I can fix it if I stick a stick through it to hold it together.

The stick makes it look better. Like it got stabbed through with a spear. No one can see there's a part missing in the back. Now I've got a real costume.

I ring a bell. I zip my jacket fast. I put the stuck-through pumpkin on my head. "Oooh, scary," says the lady who answers the door. She puts candy in my bag. I keep walking, always up the hill and over toward home, but I don't know where I am.

My candy bag is heavy. I hope the handles don't rip. Sometimes my zipper gets stuck. I stop at a house with a light on. I ring the bell. "Honey, come look," a lady calls. "It's Brom Bones."

A man comes. "Great costume, Brom," he says. They put enough candy in the bag that I can feel the weight. I don't say "Thank you" but I go "Whoooo" like a ghost. They laugh. I run to the next house.

I better go home. My jacket's getting hard to zip. My bag's so heavy it's going to break. My pumpkin's falling apart. I don't see other kids out anymore either. I wonder if I'm going the right way.

THIRTY-THIRD STREET, the sign says. I'm so smart. I knew it was this way. I just have to get to Fortieth Street and I'll know the way home.

● ● ●

One last time. I zip my jacket. I put my falling-apart pumpkin on my head. I knock. We don't give out any candy but the door flies open like somebody's waiting. Complete silence for a minute. Then they know. They start yelling.

"Du, you're crazy."

"Where have you been?"

"What are you doing? Take that thing off your head." They pull me into the house. I dump a giant pile of candy on the couch. Thuy and Lin and Vuong can't believe it. They thought something happened to me and all that happened is that I got the biggest pile of candy in the world.

Then I see my grandma sitting in the chair by the window. She's not asleep in her room. I know what she's doing. She's waiting for me. She's too worried to sleep.

"I'm okay," I say. I go to her chair. She takes my hand. "I'm okay," I repeat. "I had fun. I got a lot of candy."

"Yes, Du," she says softly. "Of course you did. And you're home now." She gets up. I help her walk to her room. It's late for her to be up. My mom and dad aren't home yet.

I come back. Thuy and Lin and Vuong have carried all the candy to the dining room table. They're putting it into piles of different kinds. They can't believe I got so much for free.

"Who's Brom Bones?" I ask. They don't know.

"I'm Brom Bones," I shriek at them.

"Oh Du, go to bed," says Thuy, laughing.

"I'll go with you next year," says Vuong.

A Surprise in the Shed

I hear guys in my class talk about going to the park sometimes. Maybe I'll go over and see if anybody's there. It's
somewhere over on the other side of school. I'll go through
the alleys. If I had my bike I'd ride over there in a second.

It's a long way to come but the park's so big I have to run
around all these little sidewalks to see the whole thing. Lots
of families are here on Sunday. My dad works harder than
anybody. He doesn't even take Sunday off. I don't see anybody from school.

Eight tennis courts and every one has people playing on

it and waiting to play on it when the others get off. The park must end here behind this tennis court. It looks like nobody ever comes to this steep canyon with no path. It's more fun to climb around here than look at baseball fields and tennis courts. I wonder if there's water in the bottom, maybe a little stream with frogs and fish. It's steep and slippery but I can get down.

A tennis ball. Practically new. I bet someone hit it over the fence and was too lazy to come down here looking for it. Here's another one, not as new but still good. . . . They're all over the place. I can't believe it. People just leave them here. I'll tie the ends of my jacket sleeves and use it for a bag.

I've got so many I'm only collecting really good ones now. I'll take them up and sell them to people waiting for a tennis court.

"Want to buy a tennis ball? It's like new. Only fifty cents." The guy takes it and bounces it. It bounces fine.

"No way, kid. Where'd you get that?"

I nod my head toward the canyon. I ask a guy waiting for another court. "If you're grabbing those when they fly over the fence you better be careful not to grab any of mine," he says. He turns to his friend and laughs. "The kid's stealing tennis balls and selling them back to us. Quite a business."

Stealing again! I didn't steal them. I wish I was back in the Philippines. I'd give every kid their own tennis ball. I'll take them home and think of what to do with them.

123

I know that kid in the yard up ahead. I don't know his name but he's in the smart kids' class at school. He was with his dad in the market the day I tried to get the free chickens. I don't know if he knows me but I'll go see if he wants a tennis ball.

Too bad. He went in the backyard. He doesn't throw so good anyway. I've seen him at recess. Nobody wants him on a team, like me, only I can throw. They just don't know it. I'll go down the alley and see if he wants to have some fun.

This is his garage because it's the same color as the house. This'll be fun. I won't say anything. I'll just throw a tennis ball over his garage and see if he throws it back. I bet he will.

Right over. Dead center in his yard.

He's not throwing it back. Maybe he didn't see it or can't throw that far. I'll try again. I can hear voices. I'll try three more and if they don't come back I'll stroll around and let him know it was me. Maybe we can throw and catch out front for a while.

One!

Two! What happened? Somebody's screaming. It sounds like a baby. It's really screaming. I wonder if I hit a baby with the tennis ball. I didn't know there was a baby there.

"Hey, you! Come here." It's the kid's dad with his long hairy beard running out from behind the garage. There's the kid too. The baby's still crying. The dad sounds so mad. I'm getting out of here.

I don't want these tennis balls anyway. My dad'll say I stole them too. I'll just dump them in the trash and go home.

●●●

"Better lock up your bike or Du Du will steal it," yells Jorge at the bike rack.

I hate school. Veronica stands in front of the room to give her speech with big sad cow eyes. Her speech doesn't have an ending. She just stops after a while and sits down. Mrs. Dorfman calls on me. I just sit there staring back at her like an American kid. She stares back over her glasses for a second, then flicks her eyes away. She calls on Tiffany. I don't have to give a speech because I won't talk. It's fun to see how scared everybody is when they go up to speak. Even Anthony. Especially Anthony. I slouch back in my chair and stare at him with a little smile. He tries to look away but his eyes keep coming back to me. He forgets his speech. "That will be enough, Anthony," says Mrs. Dorfman. I will have a bad report card but my dad doesn't expect me to have a good report card like Thuy and Lin and Vuong. He might not even look at mine. He'll just tell my mom to sign it like he did with the little practice report card Mrs. Dorfman sent home earlier. My grandma says it's because I'm new here. Thuy and Lin and Vuong started school when they were little. I'll be better later, maybe. Right now school is too boring.

●●●

"Boys and girls, this afternoon we're going to the auditorium," announces Mrs. Dorfman. "Line up outside, please."

125

I push outside fast to get away from Veronica. "Du! Du!" Mrs. Dorfman calls from the front of the line. She snaps her fingers and points to my place behind Veronica. Anthony and Jorge laugh.

Everybody's talking as we walk in the auditorium. It smells like lunch. The teachers climb up on the stage. Anthony spits a wad of paper from his mouth on my chair. I flick it back at him like shooting marbles. Kids around yell and jump out of the way even though I aim it at Anthony. Mrs. Dorfman is on the stage with the other teachers. They have piles of stuff covered with red cloth up there too. With everybody watching she points at me, stabbing the air with her finger. She stabs toward the seat at the end of the aisle. I go because I don't want to go to the Counseling Center. I want to see what's under the red cloth. Kids giggle and stick out their legs while I push down the row. I'm glad I have to move. Now I don't have to sit next to Veronica. Everybody moves one seat over. Now Anthony sits next to her.

Mrs. Dorfman smiles her big fake smile. "You all know why we're here," she announces. I don't, I say to myself just to show she's wrong. "It's that time of year. Time for gifts and goodies and the fifth-grade Christmas program." The other teachers glance at her. "Er . . . the fifth-grade winter holiday program," she adds. "We'll ask for volunteers for each of the holiday parts. The rest of you will be singing holiday songs at your seats, the angel chorus." Everybody laughs at the way she says "angel chorus." I glance down my row. Something's going on but the teachers don't notice. They're happy about the program.

Another fifth-grade teacher steps forward. Her kids all clap. "The first holiday is Hanukkah." As she says it she pulls out a candle thing from under the red cloth. "This is a holiday for . . . people of the Jewish persuasion. Do we have any children who know about Hanukkah?" Everybody looks around. I guess we don't have any because no one raises a hand. "Remember," she goes on. "Anyone may volunteer. Hanukkah lasts eight days and the children light a candle and receive a present each day." Hands shoot up all over the auditorium. I raise my hand. Eight presents! She chooses five kids from her class. It's okay with me. When they go on the stage they don't get any presents at all. They just sing a little song about something. I don't know what it is. They have to wear dumb little hats and hold fake candles.

The next holiday is called Kwanzaa and it's for black kids. Ms. Whipple from the Counseling Center comes in to talk about it. She's nice so I raise my hand but I'm the only one. No one calls on me. They call on Damian, who's black and who didn't raise his hand. He's mad. "I don't do any Kwanzaa," he says, and shrugs. "I do Christmas. We get a big tree." Finally they get some black girls to do Kwanzaa. They stand with posters and talk. Boring.

I look down the row again. Something is going on. I see Anthony and Jorge slouched down in their chairs. They're throwing something to each other behind Veronica. She's flapping around trying to grab it. Anthony and Jorge look up at the stage while they throw it so the teachers won't know.

Mr. Unger, the smart kids' teacher, grabs a hammer thing and crashes it down on the stuff under the red cloth.

Bong! Everybody jumps and laughs. "Chinese New Year!" His voice booms out. "Dragons! The beginning of a new year. A time for celebration, firecrackers, feasts . . ." I get excited as I figure out what he's talking about. It's the same as Vietnamese New Year, except we call it Tet. I was in the Philippines for the last one. I remember it was the Year of the Rat, 4681. We were way ahead there. They were only at 1984 here. Everybody shot off firecrackers. I asked my sister Lin what it's like here. She told me my mom and dad go to work as usual but when they come home some of my aunts and uncles come over and play cards. She says that's the only time all year that my dad gambles money and drinks whiskey. She said they give money to the kids in little red envelopes but I never got any in the Philippines. If I did I would give it to my grandma.

Mr. Unger hits the gong again. He pulls off the red cloth. There are a bunch of big cardboard boxes tied together and painted green and red and yellow to look like a dragon. The head has big teeth and fire from the nose and streamers like a lion's mane. He pulls out two gongs. Almost everybody raises their hand to be a dragon or hit the gongs. I raise mine too. "The dragon represents prowess, nobility and fortune to the Chinese," announces Mr. Unger, "so be sure that fits you." I don't know what those words mean but my grandma always says I'm a dragon. I wave my hand around. He chooses some kids. "And you . . . ," he calls, pointing at me. I go up on the stage with the other kids. I act like it's no big deal but I feel like kids in my class do when they give speeches. It's scary. I'm the last one up there. Mr. Unger points to the last box. I hear kids laugh. I have to bend over inside the box and I can't see anything. We jump around a little bit just to see how it works. I get pulled around behind the others. The box smells like gum. "A practice run," says Mr. Unger.

We go back to our seats. I hear whispers down the row. "Dragon Butt Du Du" I hear. Kids laugh and pass it on. I hate school.

Another teacher steps forward. "And last but not least, Christmas!" Everyone already knows about that. Everyone's hand goes up before the teacher says anything else. Except mine. The teacher tells about the spirit of giving. It takes a long time. "Who wants to be Santa Claus?" she cries, sweeping up the Santa Claus suit from the last box. Everyone starts blurting. The teacher puts up her hands. "I'll pick someone who knows how to behave," she says. It gets very quiet. "Of course, we all know this isn't the *real* Santa Claus," she whispers. She picks Alex from our class because he's fat. Everyone laughs. Alex waves and says, "Ho ho ho." I glance down the row. Veronica is blubbering in spite of the "ho ho ho." Anthony and Jorge are slouched down looking up at the stage. They have mean little smiles.

I'm thinking about what the teacher said. "This isn't the *real* Santa Claus." I can't get this figured out. "Is Santa Claus real?" I ask Jordan, the kid sitting next to me. He's a quiet kid who doesn't say much. This time he does.

He snorts with laughter. "Hey, everybody," he whispers down the row. "Du thinks Santa Claus is real." Kids laugh. They roll their eyes. I feel my face get hot. It was a stupid

129

thing to ask. Why did I let myself talk? I want to tell them that in Tet the year is already over 4000. Everybody is way behind here.

We're on our way back to class. I catch up to Mrs. Dorfman at the front of the line. "I don't want to be in the dragon," I tell her. I tell her loud so she knows I mean it.

"If that's your choice, Du," she answers, with her lips tight together after she speaks. I don't want to walk up front with her. I wait for the end of the line. Blubbery Veronica passes by me. Rosaria's got her arm around her. Veronica's holding two parts of her dumb little pink bear with the stuffing coming out. I guess that was what Anthony and Jorge were throwing back and forth. She can't tell on them because she's not supposed to bring toys to school.

On the way home I think about Santa Claus. I've heard someone say on television that Santa Claus is real. The teacher said it too. All the kids, even in fifth grade, talk about Santa Claus. They say he doesn't give toys to bad kids. It wasn't so dumb to ask if he was real. They think I'm dumb no matter what I do.

I open the door to our house. Wonderful smells come from the kitchen. I know what it means. My grandma feels good enough to cook. In the kitchen there is a plate piled with round golden buns. I know they are filled with vegetables and pork chopped into tiny bits. Those are the kind we sold in the Philippines if we could get the stuff to make them. People bought them so fast. I reach out my hand. "Not that one," my grandma says, coming into the kitchen.

She hands me a bun that is not as round or golden. It tastes just as good. She is putting on her hat like she is going off to work in the sun. She covers the plate that has the perfect buns with a paper towel. "Come, Du," she says. Where are we going with a plate of buns? She never goes out of the yard. I follow her down the front walk and out the gate.

We're going to the old spy man's house! I do not want to go. We paid him back with food already for telling about the bike. We don't have to feed him forever. "No, Grandma, no," I plead. I grab her sleeve but she shakes my hand off. That old man's going to think we're crazy. He'll just throw the buns away because they're not from Burger King. He'll think he's better than us because we bother him all the time. I stand back with my head down. He comes to the door.

My grandma pushes the plate to him. I glance up. He looks bothered. He doesn't take the plate. "You . . . call . . . school." Grandma talks in her English. "About Du." I know just what he's going to say and I'm right.

"What?" he says. I know I'm there to help her with English but I can't. I can't ask him for help. I can only look down. I wish this was over.

"You call school about Du," she repeats slowly. I know she's practiced this at home. It's all she can say. She pushes the plate at him.

"Du what?" he says.

She points at me. "Du," she repeats. My grandma doesn't know I took apart his lawn mower and gave away his oranges.

131

"Oh, him." The old man laughs. I want to run home. Everybody laughs as soon as they hear *Du*. "You want me to tell them at school that he didn't steal the bike?"

My grandma looks at me. "Du," she says sharply. She wants to know what he says.

"Yeah," I whisper. "That's what she wants but you don't have to."

"Certainly, madam," answers the old man. Who does he think he is, talking like that? I don't even know exactly what he said but I know it means yes. He takes the plate. She bows. I would like to disappear completely. Then the old man bows back. Finally we go home.

My grandma knows me. She knows I hated going over there but she made me go anyway. I throw myself down in front of the TV. "Why, Du?" she says in Vietnamese as she takes off her hat. "He is a nice man."

"Everybody laughs at me." I think about Dragon Butt Du Du and the thing about Santa Claus and the dumb reading group and being chosen last for teams.

"Everybody, Du?" she asks softly.

"Yeah, everybody," I say. She smiles at me. I think, well, anyway Jorge and Anthony, and they make other kids laugh. And Jordan laughed today about Santa Claus. "The teacher thinks I'm a troublemaker," I add.

"Do you make trouble for her?" asks my grandma. We both know the answer.

● ● ●

The principal comes to our class right when it's time to go out for PE. We wiggle around in our seats because we don't want to use up our PE time listening to him. "I have something very important to tell you," he says. He waits for a long time until we all sit still and look at him. "I have something to warn you about," he says. We settle back. This is going to take a while. I look out the window. PE isn't much fun but it's better than this. "Someone in your class has made a very serious accusation against another person in your class. A criminal accusation."

Big words. Everybody knows who he means. Everybody looks sideways at me and Veronica, except the principal. Why doesn't he just say who it is? I get ready for more trouble. I stare straight ahead now.

"I have just found out from a very reliable source that this accusation is totally false. The person accused is entirely innocent." He stops for a long time and everyone is quiet but eyeballs are moving. "From now on," he continues, "I would like everyone to think very carefully before they take chances with the reputation of a fellow classmate. Defamation of character, which means telling bad, untrue things about people, such as accusing them of stealing, is a very serious charge." He pauses with his finger tapping the air. He looks straight at Veronica. "I hope I'm understood."

I don't understand all his big words but I know what he means. That old man must have come to school and told him about the bike. I bet he feels stupid making me write all those lines and calling my dad.

"I want you all to remember the Golden Rule of life and

of our school," he adds as he finally heads for the door. "Do unto others as you would have them do unto you."

I hear Anthony snicker, "Do, do, Du Du." He's so stupid he can't think of any other joke.

At PE I feel pretty good because we play dodgeball. Nobody can ever get me out even when they team up and try to peg me. I'm too fast. I think about what the principal said and look at Veronica. Funny. Now she's in trouble because of me after all those times the other way. She looks like she's going to cry because everyone knows the principal was talking to her. She thinks she's Miss Goody-goody. When the ball rolls her way she just hands it to Rosaria. She's easy to get out anyway because she's so slow. The principal was blaming her in front of the whole class. She's not used to being in trouble. I wonder what it's like living in her house with all those big tough brothers.

● ● ●

Cat is going to like this. I got her two shrimps and a fish head. I wiped the sauce off the shrimps. She doesn't like hot sauce. I wonder where she is. She's usually back here or in the alley waiting for me. I hope that old man didn't see her and throw something at her. He thinks she has rabies.

I better look in the shed even though she doesn't usually go there in the day. She gets in through that cracked board in the back where there's a little hole. I'm surprised she can still squeeze in now that she's so fat. The board over the little window is starting to split from me dropping it all the time. I'll find a new one on Saturday.

There you are, Cat. Lying in here in the dark. Can I pet you today?

What are those? You've got kittens!

How little they are. With their faces all squished up and their eyes closed. Five I see. Two yellow, three gray like you. Your tail is twitching. You don't like me to touch them. Here, I'll watch them while you eat these shrimps. That old man just mowed his lawn. He won't mow it again for two weeks because it's winter. I'll help you hide them when he comes for the mower. We don't want him to find them. Now I've got six pets. I'll have to find a way to get more food.

● ● ●

Lin is nicer to me now because I helped her with her little plants. She still orders me around but she doesn't sound so bossy. I never do what she says anyway. When I come in from feeding Cat she's so nice that I start to wonder if she wants something. She does.

"Du, can you find me some dead bees?" she asks. This is funny. Why does Lin want dead bees? She doesn't even know it's funny.

"Sure," I say but I don't ask why because I can see she's so excited that she's going to tell me anyway.

"I tried to get some but I was afraid I'd get stung and I squished them with the flyswatter so they're no good and now I need them by tomorrow," she says.

This time I can't stop myself. She's got me interested. "Why?" I ask.

"I need to make bee sticks," she explains. "I glue the dead bee on a toothpick and rub it across the flowers, and then pollinate the glabrous ones and the hairy ones just with plants that are like them. I have to keep them apart now that they have flowers, and there are only two days when it will work. Dead dry bees are best." She shows me her little plants with their new flowers.

"I'll be right back," I say. I know where there's an empty building where I let my little skunk go and I know it has a bee nest because I've see the bees going in and out under the roof.

Here's a dead bee just where I thought there'd be some. I have to crawl around the side of the alley to spot others in the weeds and glass and trash.

I jump up like a cricket when a car honks right next to my head. It's my dad coming home down the alley in his car. "Get in," he orders, leaning over to the window. I only have about five bees but I'd get in even if I didn't have any. "Why are you crawling around in the alley like a bum? You should be doing your homework like the others. Are you going to live in the alley picking up trash for a living?"

I know he's had another bad day with Mr. Vronsky and I know he doesn't want an answer to his questions so I keep quiet.

When we go in our house, he just says, "You go wash," with his nose wrinkled up like I smell from the alley. I drop the paper towel with five dead bees in it on Lin's book when I walk by on my way to the bathroom. I'm angry because my dad finds something bad about everything I do and I'm sad too because I know he's disappointed in me. Now he doesn't even talk to me much like he does to the others. I don't know what to say to him either.

When I wash up and go in the kitchen I hear him yell at me again. "Du, you come here." I slouch into the dining room to hear what I've done wrong now. "Lin told me how you helped her with her science project. She said you found some . . . hairy plants or something when nobody else knew what the teacher wanted. She said you were helping her more just now in the alley. Why don't you say so?" He laughs and points at the paper towel. "Dead bees," he adds, shaking his head. I can't tell him that I'm afraid to talk to him when he's angry because I don't know for sure why he's angry. I don't even want to say to him that he looks angry. Lin has told him everything, though, about the plants and he's happy now. She told him no one else found mutants, just us, and that makes him happiest of all, to be better than everybody. "See, you're doing the best work for high school. How come you don't do good work for your school?" There it is again. I'm good right now but still there's something that should be better. I shrug and go watch TV.

The Dragon

School is always boring but today it's so boring I think I'm going to die. "I have some very discouraging news," announces Mrs. Dorfman in the morning. "We have fallen three units behind in social studies." She stops to let us think how terrible this is. I don't think it's terrible because I don't ever listen to social studies. The book doesn't even have good pictures. "We can't let this happen!" She stops again. Kids in the back are rolling their eyes and dragging out their books. "Today will be Social Studies Day!" There are groans. One of the groans is from me.

She calls the kids from the high reading group up to the front. They read out of the social studies book while she works at her desk. Sometimes she looks up. She pulls a card from her deck of cards with our names on them. "Read the next sentence, please," she asks the kid whose name is on the card. She puts a star next to the kid's name if they know where we are in the book. Once she pulls out a card and just puts it on the bottom of the deck. Kids sneak looks at me. She knows I'll just shrug. I don't care about stars.

I think I'll blow up into pieces, I'm so bored. I even decide to beg for the bathroom pass. But I'm saved. "I think we're all getting a little antsy, aren't we?" Mrs. Dorfman stands up. I don't know *antsy* but I see kids lift their heads and look hopeful. "You've been such wonderful listeners. We'll all go out for a game of Perimeter before practice for the . . . winter holiday program," she says.

Perimeter sounds like a dumb math kind of game but it has to be a lot better than social studies. We stuff our social studies books in our desks while she talks over the noise. She starts with "As you know" like she does all the time and I don't know but neither do a lot of other kids.

"As you know, the edge of the blacktop is the perimeter . . ."

Good, it's not math; we're going outside.

"One student will be the Perimeter Master. The rest of you will try very hard not to let the Perimeter Master tag you."

We'll be running around. Great. The Perimeter Master will never catch me.

"The first two students caught are the perimeter

assistants. They'll help the Perimeter Master until everyone is caught. Anyone else who is caught sits on the perimeter until the game is over. Last one caught is the new Perimeter Master."

Everyone is waving their hands to be the Perimeter Master. Except me. If she chooses me I'll just walk around with my hands in my pockets and not catch anyone and we'll be able to stay out all day. But she won't choose me. She smiles at the waving hands. "I'll use the cards," she says, holding up the deck. It's suddenly quiet while she pulls out a card. "Veronica." She calls out the name. Everyone else groans or laughs because Veronica'll never catch anyone except maybe Rosaria, who's as slow as she is. I'm happy. It's just like choosing me. The game'll last forever. Mrs. Dorfman's taking her work and her chair out today so she wants it to last long too.

● ● ●

Veronica's chugging around all sweaty already but she can't catch anyone. Anthony and Jorge sneak up really close to her. She lunges at them. They run away backward and she still can't catch them. The teacher's head is down looking at her papers.

"Hey, Beefaroni, Beefaroni, catch me," Anthony yells, darting past her. She doesn't even try. Beefaroni is like Du Du. I lean down with my back to her and untie and tie my shoe. I take my time. She comes up and whops me on the back. "I got you," she pants. Kids laugh. They think she caught me because I'm dumb.

"Showtime," I say softly to myself. Anthony yells "showtime" when he thinks he'll get me out in four-square. I go after him. He's fast but he's not as fast as me. I get him cornered near the wall-ball backstop. I almost whack him when I remember. I don't want him to be the second assistant. He might like that.

"Hey, Dude," yells Todd. "You can't get me." Dude, he says. He doesn't call me Du Du even though we're far away from the teacher. Dude is a good name. I go after him. He's big but he's not slow. He laughs when I catch him. Together we herd six kids including Anthony along the perimeter near the swing set. We tag them all. Veronica plods over too and gets somebody. They all have to sit down. Todd and I race for the others on the far side with Veronica puffing along behind. We clear the whole blacktop in a few minutes. The teacher looks up from her papers. "Last one out is the new Perimeter Master," she calls. We start running around all over again. It's fun.

● ● ●

The winter holiday program practice is boring. I wish it was over so I could go home and see Cat and her kittens. Everybody who didn't get a special part like me is in the angel chorus. We sit in our regular seats. We get stapled papers with the words to the music. We're supposed to share but I just give mine to Jorge. I don't want to sing about stupid reindeer that fly. When the Tet part comes, the dragon comes out like it's afraid. It walks like a cow. I kind of wish I was back in the last dragon box so I could kick around a little.

The wall clock shows five minutes until time to go home. *Beep! Beep! Beep!* blares from the wall speaker. We jump in our seats. Kids laugh and look around. *Beep! Beep! Beep!* It won't stop. It's the duck and cover signal we practice in class. Veronica and Rosaria scrunch down but there's no room under the seats. Kids are laughing because no one knows what to do. Anthony does a handstand with his head in the row and his feet waving around. Everybody laughs. The teachers hurry around whispering to each other. The dragon onstage sinks down to the floor.

The principal hurries in. "Stay calm, everybody. Stay in your seats!" he shouts. Right in the middle the beeper stops and he's still shouting. We laugh. He looks nervous. "This is not a practice." He's still shouting but not as loud. "There is a SWAT-team action in the neighborhood. We will stay at school until the all clear sounds."

"I gotta get my little brother."

"I got basketball practice."

"My mom's waiting for me." Kids all yell at once. The principal raises his hand for the quiet sign. He yells above the voices. "I'm counting on you fifth graders to set an example for the school." I don't know how we can set an example. There's nobody in here but fifth graders. I wonder what's going on outside. I wish there was a window so I could see.

"You may sit quietly in your seats," he continues. "Ms. Plinsky will lead you in singing some songs." That's hard too, sing and be quiet. Ms. Plinsky starts singing "Sweet Betsy from Pike." It's a social studies song but it's not bad. It's about people who roll around on the ground because they're hungry and thirsty. But nobody sings with Ms. Plinsky because no one knows the words. The songbooks are all in the classrooms. Now kids are getting really antsy, as Mrs. Dorfman says. I feel very antsy. One kid starts to cry because he's supposed to be home by three-fifteen, no matter what. I wonder what happens to him if he's late. Ms. Plinsky goes away to look for music.

Mr. Unger, the teacher of the smart kids' fifth grade, leaves his smart kids and vaults onto the stage. "Mental math," he shouts with his fist in the air. "My class challenges the rest of you to a mental math competition." He explains it while the other teachers tear the Christmas song sheets into strips and pass one out to everybody. Someone goes over to the media room to get library pencils. The pencils are short and don't have any erasers so no one will steal them. We each get one. We put our names on our papers. Mr. Unger will shout out math problems and we just put the answer on our paper. If we try to work the problem on the paper we're out of the contest. Usually I don't do this stuff but today I think I will. In the Philippines I helped my grandma sell food she cooked. We didn't have paper or pencil or anything but our heads there when we made change. No cash register. No calculator. Just a blanket or a table under a tree. Lots of people came. Her spring rolls and her soup with vegetables and noodles were so good people pushed around us to get some before we ran out. I had to do the money fast and right.

Mr. Unger yells, "Fire up your brains. Here we go. No talking. Just write the answers. Eight times eight hundred." Groans from my row. I write the answer. "One third of fifteen." I see Anthony's down my row writing the problem on his paper. He's erasing it with a pencil he had in his pocket. He's already behind. He can't do math no matter how he cheats. Mr. Unger starts going faster. The problems get harder. I see kids near me quit. We get to number thirty. "Seven times three hundred forty. Write. Okay? Stop!" Mr. Unger yells to pass the papers to the end of the row. "If they're late you're out. One, two, three." He runs down the aisle collecting the papers. "Who didn't miss a beat?" he yells as he runs back up the aisle. Most of the kids in his smart class shoot their hands up in the air. No one else does. He smacks his fist into his hand. "Way to go," he yells. He's proud of them. I kind of wish I was in his class. "And now . . . ," he yells, jumping back on the stage. He stops because the all clear bell rings. He laughs. "And now we'll all go home," he yells over the sound of kids. "You've been great. Have a great afternoon." Mrs. Dorfman is grabbing Alex because he's running. I go home to see Cat. Todd walks out with me.

"See ya, Dude," he says at the bike rack.

"See ya," I say.

I see some police cars on Fortieth Street on my way home. I hear people saying that a man robbed a store but there's nothing to see now. If he robbed the store when I was

144

coming home from school maybe I would have caught him. I'd be on television and the kids at school would see it.

● ● ●

At home everything is crazy. My sister Lin is crying because she got a B on a test. She never gets anything but As. My dad slams in the front door. Is he mad because Lin got a B? "You kids are gonna do it whether you want to or not!" he yells. Do what? He's yelling at Thuy and Lin and Vuong. This is interesting. I sneak in to listen.

"My friends'll see me," Thuy mutters. "I have to study."

"It's so early. We won't be able to do anything else all day."

"It hardly pays anything." I never heard them argue with him before. Their voices are soft like they almost don't dare to have him hear.

My dad's fist slams down on the table. The heavy books jump. "When they call we say yes. And that's that!" Thuy and Lin and Vuong all look down at the table but they don't say yes. My dad stands staring at the tops of their heads. Maybe for the first time they won't do what he wants. "That's that," he repeats. He slams out the door to go back to work.

I ask Vuong when he comes to watch TV. "He wants us to get up at four in the morning to deliver Sunday papers," he tells me. "It pays about nothing. Thuy told him no on the phone and he came running home."

"How come he wants to do it if it pays nothing?" I ask. I

145

know my dad doesn't leave work and come running home for nothing.

"Well, it pays a little bit but not enough to get up at four a.m.," complains Vuong. "He'll make us save all the money anyway."

"For what?" I ask. My dad never buys the stuff you see on TV.

"He wants to send us to college and buy a house," answers Vuong like it's something he's heard from our dad over and over again.

College is more school. "I don't want to go to college and we got a house," I answer, and shrug.

"He wants to own a house, not rent one, and we want to go to college." Vuong doesn't want to talk to me about it anymore. He looks at the TV.

"Will you do it?" I ask.

"I don't want to," he answers. "Maybe they'll never call."

"You could answer the phone and say we don't want the job. He'll never know," I say. I just say it for fun but Vuong turns to look at me funny. He goes in the dining room to whisper to Thuy and Lin.

I go to look for my grandma but she's sleeping. I climb through the shed window and sit with Cat and her kittens. I scratch her chin. She purrs. The kittens wiggle around trying to get the best place to eat. I think about a place to hide them from the old man. Maybe Cat knows best.

● ● ●

My dad does look at my report card. He knows the day we get it and he asks to see it. For a minute I think I'll tell him I left it at school or lost it or something but that will just make it worse when he finds out. It's folded up into a little tiny square in my pocket. I take it out and unfold it. I hand it to him. There is a long heavy silence while he looks at each grade. He doesn't yell at me or slam anything down on the table.

"So, your teacher says you're not even trying," he says. "You're acting like a gang boy, a criminal. You're mean to people. You can't read. I don't know whose boy this is." He says it sadly like he gives up. I know the report card doesn't say all that. It has Needs Improvement checks next to "Follows classroom rules" and "Treats classmates with respect." Not respecting my classmates means I won't let Anthony call me Du Du but I don't tell my dad that. I got a U, *Unsatisfactory,* in "Effort," which means Mrs. Dorfman thinks I don't try. "Reading" is a D for dumb reading group. For him there is no excuse at all, anywhere, for a report card like this. He places the report card on the table, turns his back on me and leaves the room. Later I get my mom to sign it when she is in a hurry to leave for work.

● ● ●

Winter holiday practice again. We're going to practice every day until the day of the program. That means no PE. Before we begin Mr. Unger jumps up on the stage. He's waving the strips of math paper. "What a great job you guys

147

did!" he yells. "Give yourselves a big round of applause." Everybody claps and cheers and whistles. He doesn't get nervous like Mrs. Dorfman when it gets noisy. "Way to go!" he yells. "And now for the winners."

It gets quiet. Even kids who quit writing answers halfway through get quiet in case everybody else was even worse and they won. "Many of you got over ninety percent correct!" he yells. More cheers. "But those problems number fifteen and twenty-seven were doozies. Those are the ones that did us in." Kids groan. "Only two people got everything right because of those two ugly problems." He waits, looking all around the auditorium. Kids are squirming hopefully. "And the one hundred percent winners are . . ." His feet pound the stage like a drum. "In my phenomenal class, Iris Perez! Come on up, Iris." Kids clap, especially the ones from Mr. Unger's class, and she runs up to the stage. "And in Mrs. Dorfman's equally phenomenal class, Du Nguyen!"

There's a moment of complete silence. Nobody believes it. I don't think about winning. I feel scared. I have to run up on the stage. "Put your hands together for Du. Come on up, Du Nguyen." Kids clap then. Pretty loud, I think. Kids near me push me out of my seat. Cheering picks up in my class. We tied the smart kids' class. Because of me. I run up to the stage. Mr. Unger gives Iris and me each a new pencil. Then he snatches them back. "You two don't need these," he says, breaking off the end with the erasers. He gives the broken pencils back to us. Everybody laughs.

"Seriously," he goes on. "With the skills these two have developed I wouldn't be surprised if they end up owning the

148

pencil factory. The rest of you out there, follow their example and next time it will be you up here . . . with a broken pencil to show for your work." Kids laugh again. I laugh too. "And the winners also receive this Mental Math Champion certificate to keep so they can remember this day and what they did. Let's have another round of applause." He hands Iris and me thick papers with gold paper medals and little blue ribbons stuck on them that have our names and "Mental Math Champion" and the date in fancy printing. Everybody wants to see it when I get back to my seat. They want to see the broken pencil too.

We start the winter holiday program practice. I'm happy. I like school. I might even sing in the angel chorus just because I feel like making noise.

The Tet part of the program starts. The girl in the front box of the dragon is absent. Mrs. Dorfman asks for volunteers. I wave my hand around without thinking. "All right, Du," she says like she's sure it's a mistake. "You may have another chance."

I go up onstage again. No problem. I crawl under the front box of the dragon. It's the box with the head, a big mouth full of teeth, flames from the nose painted along the sides of the face and lots of colored streamers all around the back for the mane. I don't want the dragon to look like a cow. I grab the sides of the box. I jump into the middle of the stage. For a second the other boxes hold me back, then they jump too. I jump straight up and shake the box back and forth. Through my box I hear laughing. It's easy to act crazy when no one can see you. *Bong!* go the gongs. I leap and jump and shake and bow and go in circles until someone knocks on the box and says it's time to go offstage. I'm sweaty when I get out from under the box. I walk back to my seat. Kids are still laughing. Somebody pounds my back. "You were great, Dude," they say.

●●●

At home I show Thuy and Lin and Vuong my Mental Math Champion certificate.

"Oh, Du, now you will get As, I think."

"See, Du, you just have to get over being lazy."

"You could get everything right in spelling too if you tried."

I feel embarrassed. It's such a little thing but they pretend it's big. I wish I hadn't told them. I give my Mental Math Champion certificate to my grandma. She puts it on the chest in her room where she keeps a piece of bamboo, a little vase and a necklace from Vietnam. I don't tell my dad because he will say it was just a game or say that it proves I am a lazy boy and not trying, and to him lazy and not trying are the worst things of all.

The Counseling Center

Vuong comes up the front walk with a long box. "Whatcha got?" I yell. I hope it's something fun.

"Nothing," he says. He brings the box into the work-room. Thuy and Lin are studying. He opens the box slowly just to make me wait. He pulls out a little fake Christmas tree all folded up. It has red balls already stuck on it and it leans when he sticks it on its stand. We look down at it. So does Buddha. Thuy and Lin and Buddha laugh at Vuong. I do too. His tree is nothing like the tall shining ones on TV all covered with lights and angels. Vuong takes the tree to his room and shoves it in the corner.

I know there's no real Santa Claus anywhere but I'm not sure about Christmas. "Did they have Christmas in Vietnam?" I ask my mom.

"We're here now," she answers. She and my dad always say stuff like that when I ask questions about Vietnam. My sisters give me angry looks. They say it makes my mom sad to remember because of the war and the people in her family who died and the ones left behind that she may never see again. They don't want me to make my mom sad. I don't want to either but I would just like to know. We don't do Christmas but maybe other people from Vietnam do. My grandma tells me stories but not about what really was.

"Are there reindeer in Vietnam?" I ask my grandma. She thinks for a minute.

"No," she says. "We have water buffalo instead. Water buffalo are big with powerful shoulders and curved horns." Then she tells me a story about a tiger who sees a water buffalo work all day for a farmer. The tiger asks the buffalo why he works for a puny little man who is so much weaker than he is. The buffalo says it is because the man has a special box of wisdom. The tiger is curious and grabs the man in his claws and demands to see his wisdom. The man says yes but he is afraid if he goes to get it the tiger will eat his buffalo. "Let me tie you to this tree," he says, "so I can show you my wisdom." The tiger lets himself be tied to a tree and the man sets the tree on fire. When the ropes burn, the tiger is free

152

but he has stripes where the rope burned his fur. The tiger knows he has seen the man's wisdom.

Talking tigers are about like flying reindeer but my grandma tells me the story so I will be smart. Maybe the Santa Claus story is so kids will be good. I'm smart enough to figure out that my parents didn't have Christmas in Vietnam. The old man used to have Christmas but I can tell he hasn't used the Christmas lights and the red glittery balls in the shed for years.

The old man never found Cat and the kittens when he got his mower but if he gets his Christmas stuff he'll find her for sure. I get a little piece of a hot dog to take to Cat. She likes Vietnamese fish better but hot dog is all we have today. I snake quickly through the little window. I hear the squeaky cries. The kittens are fine but they are noisy now. They are all there in a tangle of fur pushing their paws against each other, looking for Cat. All but the littlest gray one have their eyes open now. Cat pushes her way in through the crack. I give her the piece of hot dog, which she chews quickly holding it down with one paw. There are little cries again as she steps among the kittens. They all struggle to get to her. Soon they will be ready to eat fish and hot dogs too. Where will I get enough food? How can they stay hidden? I better get out my box of wisdom and figure it out.

● ● ●

I walk to school. Christmas is everywhere. The Mexican guy's house has a big Santa in front and lights all over the porch. The gas station has white bears bigger than kids, with red Santa Claus hats. They're for sale in a big pile. The streetlights have fake wreaths on them. The window of the ninety-nine-cent store is full of Christmas candy and Christmas paper and dolls and toy cars and a lot of other junk.

I think school will be different this last week but it isn't. "Du, you're to go to the Counseling Center immediately." All the kids look at me the way they always do when someone's in trouble. But no one says, "What'd you do, Du Du?" the way they used to. I hope whatever I've done is not so bad that I miss the winter holiday program. The dragon won't be any good without me. I walk slowly over to the Counseling Center. I try to think of what I've done lately. Nothing big that I can think of but sometimes it's hard to know what they consider bad. Like the time I put glue on my arms. That didn't seem so bad and it was fun to peel it off. Mrs. Dorfman said it was a "waste of classroom materials." Other kids were wasting more glue dripping it all over their paper sculptures.

Ms. Whipple smiles when I come in. "We need your help, Du," she says. What is this about? Maybe it's a trick. "I must warn you that what I'm asking of you will be difficult. We have a mother in the nurse's office who is very upset. The nurse has found that her child has a hearing loss. The mother speaks a little English but when she heard about her child she was so upset that she can't understand anything else. I thought of you, Du. I thought you could explain to her in Vietnamese. Will you try?"

I shrug. I don't know anything about hearing loss.

"Thank you, Du. What we say in there must go no further than the nurse's office. Is that understood?"

I shrug again. Why would I tell anybody? She keeps looking at me with her eyebrows up until I say, "Yeah, I understand."

She leads me down the hall. Inside the nurse's room the nurse is talking loud and slow, holding a little paper book in her hand. A mother is holding a boy who is just a little kindergarten kid so tight that his face is squished against her shoulder. Tears run down her face. She stands up like she is ready to walk out the door. The mother sees me. She turns her back like she's hiding her kid from me. I don't like this. I wish I had not said yes. The nurse sees me too. She must have been working hard because she puffs a big puff of air like she's had enough. She will give the hard job to me. "Tell her there are things we can do to help him," she says quickly and softly. The mother sobs.

I figure this out and say it in Vietnamese. The mother cries harder. I do not want to be here. I wish I was back in spelling drill or social studies. The nurse reads something from the little book. I can't figure out what she's talking about. The mother isn't listening. The nurse reaches out with the book to show her but the mother thinks she is trying to take the kid. She backs away. I think of just clamming up or walking out the door. I think of my grandma. "You're smart, Du," she always says. It's noisy now with the nurse talking loud again and the mother crying and the kid squirming. I try to think of what my grandma would do.

"Just a minute," I say as loud as the nurse in English, and then in Vietnamese. I am surprised that it is suddenly quieter. "Can I have the book?" I ask in English. The nurse hands it to me. "What You Should Know About Hearing Loss," it says on the cover, with a picture of an ear. I take it over to the mother. I show it to her. She looks away. I open the book. I point to the words on the first page. "Hearing loss has many causes," it says. Then it tells about each one. I point at the words. I tell her as close as I can what they say. She looks down at the book. At least it is a lot quieter in here but she is still squishing her kid. I turn the page. Some of the words I don't know but I tell her pretty much what it says.

She is listening. It is quiet now except for me talking in Vietnamese. I don't talk at school much and I never talk Vietnamese at school. I get to the part about hearing aids to put in kids' ears. The kid struggles free. The mother lets him go. She's crying again. She shakes her head about the hearing aids. She knows that people will see them and then everybody will know that something is wrong with her child. I think of my grandma again.

"It's better than not hearing," I say. That's not in the book. The book says that children who can't hear won't do well in school or learn how to talk right. I finish the last page of the hearing loss book. The nurse asks me to tell the mother about a doctor appointment. She gives the mother the book even though she can't read it. Ms. Whipple has been waiting in the doorway. She walks with me out to the playground where recess is just starting.

"You did that beautifully, Du," she says. I look around to

make sure no one heard *beautifully*. I don't want kids to start calling me Beautiful Du Du. "Isn't it time you showed Mrs. Dorfman that you can read?" she asks. I shrug. "You have to give everyone a chance," she says. "Even your teacher."

This is funny. She wants me to give Mrs. Dorfman a chance? I wonder how she knows I don't want to do anything my teacher wants me to do. Ever since she put me in the dumbest groups and didn't hear when kids called me Du Du. I'll have to think about it.

"I'll see you in the dragon," calls Ms. Whipple. She hurries back to the Counseling Center, where the playground aide is arriving followed by three kids who don't look happy. I run off to recess but I'm thinking about the sad mother in the nurse's office. She's right. Her kid's life will be miserable if he has hearing aids sticking out of his ears. Some kids will make fun of him. But then most kids won't. I won't. I think of Todd calling me Dude instead of Du Du and letting me share his bike lock. I'd much rather be like Todd than like Anthony. I'm going to watch for that kid on the kindergarten playground and do something to make him feel good.

Lightning

Everybody's excited. The last day before Christmas vacation. "Oops!" Mrs. Dorfman would say. "You mean winter vacation." It's weird. She doesn't want us to say *Christmas* even though we all make paper stockings with cotton ball trim and the custodian dresses like Santa Claus and puts candy canes and erasers in them before recess.

It's time for the winter holiday program. I'm just a little scared when I see everybody's mom and dad in the audience. People are crowded in the back and around the sides. My mom and dad are at work. They don't have time for stuff like this. My grandma can't walk over here by herself. "You remember everything, Du," she said, "and tell me about the wonderful dragon." I sit in a room behind the stage with the rest of the dragon. We listen to Hanukkah and Kwanzaa and make faces at each other to show we're kind of nervous. I'm just scared for a moment when I see how many people are out there. I crawl under my box and wait for the gong. At the sound we all leap from behind the side curtain. I hear laughing and clapping. Hearing it makes me jump and shake and whirl around even fiercer than before. They can't see me in the dragon box but I can hear them laughing. They clap louder than they did for the others. I feel great when the last gong signal sounds and we jump back behind the curtain. I stick the dragon's head out from behind it one more time and give my mane a big shake. People laugh and clap. I wish I could do it again. The audience likes Santa Claus too, especially when he has to hold up his pants and his beard falls off. At the end of the winter holiday program Mr. Unger calls everybody back to the stage. When he says our names we crawl out from under the dragon and the people clap again. We go back to our classroom, where some of the moms and dads have set up a party with red and green cupcakes and punch and candy canes.

"You're some dragon," one of the dads says.

"A cupcake for a dragon," says a mom as she puts one on my desk.

Everyone yells "Merry Christmas" as we leave school after the winter holiday program and the party. Why not just call it Christmas vacation? Winter sounds like cold and snow and it's warm enough I don't even need a jacket. When I get home I tell my grandma everything. I tell her how everybody knows now that I'm a dragon.

• • •

I get up early because there's no school. I feed Cat a piece of chicken I saved and some rice. I mess around in the alley. I walk over to school. Todd is inside the playground fence shooting baskets. I climb the fence. We play basketball, which is better than baseball but not as good as soccer. Some high school kids take over the basketball hoop. We try soccer with Todd's basketball but when we kick it there's a loud thump, our feet sting and the basketball doesn't go very far. Then the school security guy kicks everybody out.

We walk down the alley. I find a long rusty strip of metal. We go to my yard to make a catapult out of the metal strip and some wood. I show him how to fold paper into a cube that holds water. We make three of the cubes so we can shoot them. We brace our catapult against the edge of the sidewalk in front. I can see the old spy watching us out of his window but the catapult isn't even aimed at his house. The cubes fly across the street. *Splat!* They land on the sidewalk. We need more ammunition but the cubes take too long to make. We go to the 7-Eleven and Todd buys little balloons. We fill them with water. We shoot them all the way across the street. Todd says "Cool, Dude" each time a balloon flies off the catapult.

"Hey, look, here comes a target," Todd yells. Two kids

from Mr. Unger's smart kids' class are riding their bikes down my street. We duck down. We wait until they're close. We shoot two water balloons real fast. One balloon splashes in front of them; the other hits the back kid in the leg. "Gotcha!" yells Todd, jumping up. I jump up too. They see us and ride away fast.

Todd runs across the street to grab one of the balloons. It didn't break when it hit. I get him in the back while he's leaning over. He throws his balloon at me but he misses because a car goes by. He hits the car. *Screech* go the brakes. A guy jumps out. We run.

We run down to the corner and back through the alley. We see the guy drive away. I run to get the catapult. *Whoosh!* Something wet hits me right in the head. "Ha ha ha!" I hear. It's the smart kids. They took our catapult. They've got a plastic bag full of ammunition plus the stuff we left behind. Todd and me make a plan behind a parked car. I run and yell at them from across the street. They're busy shooting at me. Todd sneaks behind them and grabs our bag of ammunition. We peg them from across the street. Throwing's faster than using the catapult. They grab their ammunition and run for the alley. We hide in the alley behind some garbage cans and wait. They come sneaking along looking for us. We jump up from behind the cans and score direct hits. They come after us. We all run up and down the alley hiding behind garages and trash cans. We throw balloons whenever someone runs from their cover. Sometimes the balloon doesn't break. Then I throw their own ammunition back at them. I score more direct hits.

We run out of ammunition so we all go back to my yard. My grandma taps on the window. I go see what she wants. She gives me a big plate of spring rolls and cans of soda to take to the guys in the backyard. Everybody likes the spring rolls. We try to see who can eat the most hot sauce. The smart kids' names are Gil and Martin. I run inside to get my Halloween candy. It was fun to get it but I don't like to eat most of it. I dump it out on the stairs for them.

"You still have Halloween candy?" They sort through the pile. They eat some.

"Who's Brom Bones?" I ask. They shake their heads. Then Gil looks up.

"I know who he is," he says. "He's in a book about a guy who scares a schoolteacher by making it look like his head's cut off. He puts a scary-looking pumpkin on his head."

Great! "He scares a schoolteacher?" I ask to be sure.

"Yeah, the teacher runs right out of town and is never seen again." I decide I'll be Brom Bones next Halloween too.

I think of showing them Cat and her kittens but I don't because I know the old man is watching us. He might find out about her even if we all go through the side window. Besides, I think the other guys are too big to get through. Gil's got some cards. We play cards sitting on the stairs. Everyone has different rules. Todd and Gil and Martin have to go home because it's getting late.

I don't want the day to end. The battle with the balloons was so cool and being with those guys having fun instead of being in school was like the Philippines. I used to think that it would always be different in America. I never see Thuy and Lin and Vuong messing around with friends. I don't want to go just sit inside now so I walk down to the Mexican guy's house when I see him out in front. I hold a flashlight for him while we look far down in the truck engine. Once he has me reach in and turn a metal thing. He can't reach it because his hands are too big. His wife calls him in to answer the telephone so I go home.

● ● ●

"Du, Du," Lin is yelling from the back door. I've been up for hours. I visited Cat and her kittens. I fed her. I watched TV. I ran over to school to see if anyone was playing basketball. I helped some guys start a car by pushing it down the street. I did some other stuff and Lin and Thuy and Vuong just got up. They're the lazy ones.

"Yeah, sleepyhead," I say like Mrs. Dorfman. Lin jumps because she didn't see me right next to the back porch.

"Mom says you should take all the cans to the recycle place today," Lin says.

"Did she say me?" I ask quickly. They always give me the bad jobs.

"Yes, you. She said whoever wasn't doing anything and that's you."

"You're sleeping. That isn't doing anything," I answer.

"Thuy and me are going to the library and Vuong's gotta go to the market so that leaves you." Once I was really bored and I went with Thuy and Lin to the library. They sat at a big table with their friends and whispered all day. I got more

163

bored there. When I started fixing the bulletin board better the lady behind the desk got mad. I won't go to the market because I don't want to walk down the street pushing that old rattly cart we got. If kids from school see me they'll laugh. I left it once when I saw some kids coming and when I went back some of the stuff was gone. So I have to take the recycle cans.

I like squashing the cans. I do it on the front sidewalk. I jump high and land on them. I have to wear shoes or it hurts too much.

I don't like walking down the street with a big plastic bag full of squashed cans. I hope no one sees me.

"Dude, hey, wait up." It's Todd.

"Hi," I say when he rides up. "I gotta go recycle these for my sister." At least he'll know it's not for me.

"Yeah," he says. "I had to do it yesterday." I'm surprised. I didn't know American kids did this. I thought they just threw everything away and bought more.

"Wanna play basketball after?" I ask.

He shakes his head. "I got soccer practice." I wish we could have a water balloon fight like we did that day with Gil and Martin. Or play basketball or anything. I'm tired of just watching TV and messing around in the alley by myself. Maybe I can make something in the shed.

"Hey, why don't you come to practice with me?" Todd is riding circles around me with his bike while I drip soda on the sidewalk out of my leaky bag. "Coach won't mind. We only got one more game and we're almost in last place anyway."

"Okay," I say, and shrug. I wonder what it's like. He follows me to the recycle place. I wish I still had my bike.

● ● ●

Todd rides his bike slow and I run along beside. His soccer practice is at the high school field. Not just his team but a whole bunch of teams, even girls' teams, are practicing there. It's all divided up with orange plastic things and soccer balls flying everywhere. I never came here before. Now I know where all the kids go all the time.

Todd drops his bike on a pile of other bikes. He runs over to a tall guy in a baseball hat. I see Todd pointing at me and the tall guy looking over. I look down like I'm doing something else. When I look up Todd waves his arm for me to come over.

"This is Coach," says Todd.

"So, Du, you ever play soccer?" asks Coach. I shake my head. It's too much to say I used to kick trash balls and tires around in the Philippines and play feather birdie sometimes all day long. He'd doesn't want to hear all that.

"He's real fast," says Todd. I shrug.

"Well, we're short players because of Christmas and it's only a scrimmage today. I'll put you in sometime if one of the guys needs a rest. Okay?" he says. I shrug.

Coach has us all run back and forth through the orange things—cones, he says. We run forward and backward. He's got a whole big bag full of soccer balls. Todd and I get one and kick it to each other. A ball hits me in the back. I turn fast. I kick it on the bounce all the way across the field.

"You jerk," a guy yells at me. I guess it's his ball. I shrug but I won't do it again because I don't want to get kicked out. Gil from the smart kids' class is on Todd's team too. I see other guys from school.

The scrimmage is just like a game. The guys on one team have to take off their shirts so they can tell the teams apart. The ones with no shirts are the Skins. I'm glad Todd's team is the Shirts if I get to play. I'm skinny.

I watch from the side. Todd runs around like crazy. He kicks hard. Coach keeps yelling "Positions, positions" and "Cover that guy" and stuff like that. I can't tell what he means exactly. The other coach is yelling too. Two guys crash into each other. The Shirts guy limps off the field.

"Hey, Du. You go in on defense. Okay?" Coach kneels to look at the hurt guy's ankle.

I run on the field. The ball is at the other end so I run after it. Just as I get to it a big Skins guy kicks it way down the field. I run the other way down the field. A Skins guy is way ahead of me. He gets the ball. I'm almost up to him when he kicks the ball between the cones at the end. The Shirts guy who's supposed to stop it is mad. "He was way up at forward," he yells, pointing at me. "I can't stop everything without any defense."

Coach calls me over. "Du," he says. "I'm taking you out for a minute. When I put you back in, get the ball and put it in that goal." He points to the cones at the far end of the field. He's laughing. I guess I made a mistake. Is he laughing at me? I kneel on one knee on the side like the other Shirt who's out of the game.

I watch to see what I'm supposed to do if I go in again. I know I messed up the first time. But he said he'd put me back in. I don't want them to laugh at me. Out of the corner of my eye I see another guy walk up to Coach.

"Any score?" he asks.

"One to nothing, Skins," Coach answers. I guess the one goal was my fault but he doesn't say it. "Watch this, though, when I put this kid in, friend of Todd's, watch him run. Doesn't know the game but he's lightning."

Me? I'm lightning! I thought I was just messing up. I watch guys running up and down the field.

A Shirt trots off with his face all red. He's out of breath. "Okay, Du. Remember what I said," calls Coach. I remember. I run out after the ball. I get there but six feet are in a mess kicking it all over the place. It goes out of bounds. A Skin throws it in. I wait until it lands. Four guys get there at once. A Skin kicks it all the way down the field. I chase after it. The other guys have been running a lot. I see they're kind of tired. I get to the ball in time to kick it out. I saw Todd do that. In the Philippines we didn't have cones so it never went out. It's better to kick it out than let the Skins score. A Skins guy throws it in to another Skin. This time I don't wait for it to land. I jump in and kick it like kicking a feather birdie before it even hits the ground. Now I've got it for myself, I run. I run—like lightning, I guess—all the way down the field with the ball. Three Skins are running toward me.

"Dude, pass, over here." I hear Todd. I shoot it to him. The Skins turn too late. Todd has it. He doesn't blast it. He runs toward the goal cones like he's going to kick it right and when the guy in the cones goes right Todd bumps the ball left. It rolls in. The Shirts all jump around Todd. He runs over and slaps my hands in the air. They jump around me too. I'm glad he scored. I'm glad I ran like lightning.

The scrimmage ends at one to one because we have to give the field to another team. I'm sweaty. I'm happy. I wish it wasn't the last practice so I could come again.

"Hey, Du," Coach calls. He's got a pencil and paper. "Give me your name and number," he says. "I'll give you a call when we start practice next year. You don't want to let those feet go to waste." Todd and Gil slap me on the back.

● ● ●

When I get home it's almost dark. My dad and Vuong are just leaving for the market in the car. I go too because I'm too excited about soccer to go sit in the house. The more I think about it the more I can see that Todd and Coach and those guys thought I was good. It's a long time until soccer starts again next year. I'm going to practice all the time. Maybe Todd and Gil and Martin will want to practice too. I want to tell my dad and Vuong about it but I'm afraid my dad might say no. I'm going to ask when I'm sure he'll say yes. I have to find out if it costs any money first.

The market's busy. My dad sends me off to find onions and noodles and oil. Vuong has to get orange juice and

168

beans and flour. My dad will get the rest with the cart. Then we all meet at the checkout stand to save time. I'm there first even though I stop to smell the barbecue ribs and chicken that American people buy already cooked. I get at the end of the long line with my arms full of stuff. It's kind of funny because the kid from Mr. Unger's class with the dad with the beard is in my same line again like when I was so dumb and thought I could get free chickens. This time they're ahead of me. I remember throwing the tennis balls for him to catch too but he probably doesn't remember about that. I know now from school that his name is Andy. "Hi, Andy," I say when the kid looks my way. He turns away and whispers to his dad. I shrug. Vuong and my dad get in line with me. Some people give us mean looks because they thought it was just me in line. My dad doesn't notice. He just wants to save time.

We check out and my dad pays. To save time we all carry bags and leave the cart behind. We head for our car in the parking lot, each of us with two or three bags.

"Excuse me, sir." We turn at the sound of the sharp voice and see Andy's dad coming up behind us in the parking lot. Andy's kind of hiding behind him looking worried.

"I wonder, sir, if you realize your boy there"—the dad pauses to point at me—"is headed for some big problems later if he's allowed to continue his current behavior." My dad and Vuong and I all stand and stare at him. I know the words well enough to know he's complaining about me. He waits a minute but my dad's face is like stone. "Do . . . you . . . speak . . . English?" he asks slowly.

"Yes. What are you talking about?" demands my dad. I see anger signs growing but the bearded dad doesn't stop.

"I don't mean to interfere," he says, "but if the boy's problems can be treated now it may save you much heartache later. I have some experience in child psychology and I feel it's my duty to warn you that these early behaviors don't just disappear. They become worse over time."

My dad is impatient. "What are you talking about?" he demands again, shifting his grocery bags.

"I've seen the boy on two occasions," says the dad. "Once he was cheating the market and he ran off before they could deal with him. Another time he attacked my son in our own yard and, in fact, slightly injured his young sister. My son tells me he's in trouble often at school. You can ignore this or seek help from a child psychologist. I just feel it's my duty to warn you. Good night."

He turns and walks away. Andy scuttles around in front of him with his shoulder hunched up. My dad turns and stares at me.

"And another thing," the bearded dad calls back. "If there's any retaliation against my son by your son I will call the police immediately."

Vietnamese explodes from my dad's mouth. "What's he saying? He sees you steal from the market. You hurt this boy's sister. This is how you repay all the work we do for you?" He slams the groceries into the car. I jump in the backseat so he can't leave without me.

"I didn't steal from the market and I didn't mean to hit his sister. It was an accident. I was just—"

"You be quiet," he yells. "This man just made this all up, I suppose. All the work we do is for nothing when you act like a gang boy. I'll send you back and see how you like it."

I know now that he can't send me back but I know he would like to. I start to explain again but he is too angry to listen. Vuong makes a sign for me to be quiet. Can I explain later? I don't know if he will ever believe me. It's like some of the stuff that was on my report card, being mean to people and bad grades, and before when I lied about the bike a little. He's still angry about all that.

"You leave his son alone," my dad warns me as we drive up to the house. Now I'm angry too. I was trying to be friends with Andy by helping him learn how to throw. If my dad would just listen to my side for once—but he's always sure that whatever I'm doing is wrong or lazy or dumb. Lin says it's because more than anything he wants us to be good and make something of ourselves. I'm good at lots of things—soccer, and making stuff and fixing it, and math, and being a dragon, and taking care of my grandma. But whatever I'm good at he doesn't notice or think it's important.

After Vuong and me put away the groceries, Vuong motions me to come in his room. "What was that guy talking about?" he asks in a low voice. I tell him the whole story of the free chickens and how I ran away and about the tennis balls. Sometimes he smiles but he can see I don't like it when he does so he stops. It takes a long time because he keeps asking me questions. "Why did you run away?" he asks when I tell about the store manager and later, the baby crying. "No wonder they think you did something wrong."

I think about why I ran away. It's because of lots of things. In the market everyone was staring and the manager was talking about stealing and calling the police. It was only my second time there. When I hit Andy's little sister I didn't expect a baby to be back there or anyone to cry. I didn't even know if Andy wanted to be friends with me anyway or if he was a guy who said "Du Du" like Anthony or what the tall dad with that big beard would do to me when he came running out from behind the garage. Vuong shakes his head. I don't even know if he believes me.

"What's a child psychologist?" I ask.

Now Vuong laughs. "It's a doctor for kids who are crazy," he says. "Don't worry, though. I think it costs a lot of money to go to one. You're crazy, Du, but Dad'll never pay for it." He laughs harder. He knows I'm not crazy.

"It must be there's a *tinh* around here," I say, looking around.

Now he doesn't know. "What's a *tinh*?" he asks.

"Grandma told me about them. When you open your mouth too much a *tinh* draws out your soul. That's what makes you crazy . . . so you better keep your mouth shut."

Two Heroes

On December twenty-fourth, the day before Christmas, my mom and dad come home early. They don't have to work on Christmas because nobody works on Christmas. They'll go visit the cousins in Orange for four days. My grandma doesn't feel good enough to go so long away from home. My mom says she'll stay with her but I want to stay and also I have to feed Cat. So Grandma and me stay home. When they all get in our car with their bags and boxes I can see there's hardly enough room for all of them. We wave good-bye.

My grandma says we'll make a Christmas cake. She says it in Vietnamese except for the word *Christmas*. I know she's never made a Christmas cake before but she can cook anything. I look over at the old man's window to see if he's spying on us. His house looks just the same as it does on all the other days. Where are his presents and his tree and his jingle bells? I know where his Christmas tree lights are. They're in the shed in the trunk. I start to worry again. Maybe he just puts his tree up on the last night. He does everything slow. What if he goes in there and finds Cat? Before when he went in she must have stayed hidden in the corner under the shelf but now I hear the kittens meowing and moving around every time I go in there. Soon she won't be able to hide them. Yesterday I was making a little roller coaster out of the metal set. One of the kittens crawled halfway across the floor. What if he finds them and does something to them? Cat would be so sad. So would I. I'll watch him tonight. I know that right now he doesn't have any tree to put any lights on anyway.

Dark already. The phone rings. Nobody calls except to talk to Thuy or Lin or Vuong but I'm bored so I answer.

"I need a Mr. Nguyen," says a gruff voice. I'm curious.

"Just a minute," I say. I wait a minute. "Hello," I say. I make my voice deep.

"Yeah, Nguyen," says the voice. "Route guy quit a few hours ago. It's gotta be Sunday. Everything delivered before seven a.m. Take it or leave it." It's the man about delivering the paper. Thuy and Lin and Vuong said no but I'm sure my dad still wants it. He won't be home yet by Sunday. I bet I could do it. I could get up early and run around with a bunch of papers. It'd be fun.

"I'll take it," I say in my deep voice. He doesn't say anything for a minute.

"Is this Nguyen?" the guy asks again.

"Yeah," I say even deeper. "I'll take it."

"Okay, you got it. Route sheet and papers'll be there about three, three-thirty. Job ends for you if they're not all out by seven. Paper'll be big because of the sales. You know where to reach me if there's a problem. Okay?"

"Okay," I say. We hang up. I wonder what it's like, how many papers. Where are the houses? It's not until Sunday. I guess I'll go to bed. I could sleep on Vuong's bed tonight but I like the couch.

● ● ●

Ghosts again. No, not ghosts, fire sirens. I heard them in my dream. They sound close. I'll go see what's happening. Where are my shoes?

The fire's close. Down at the end of the alley. Those flames are high! It's the big apartments burning. It's like fireworks! Sparks are blowing all over in the wind. Everybody's out here. People wrapped up in blankets, just out of bed, staring at the fire. This is cool. I'd go up to the top of that fire truck ladder in a second. Spray water down from way up high. Two big firemen drag the hose. I'd go first and they'd give it to me to spray. Millions of sparks fly around up there.

People yell. Something caves in. I'm glad I'm not in there.

175

The firemen up there are brave, staying even with the smoke and sparks. I'm gonna get closer to see what they're doing.

• • •

Sparks everywhere. It's like Tet in the Philippines. If I stretch my neck back and squint my eyes the flames and sparks look crazy. They go in every direction.

The police won't let me get any closer. Everybody inside the police line is rushing around and yelling at each other. I think the people who lived in the apartments are the quiet ones, just staring. A family like us is there, four kids and a mom and dad, huddled up with their arms around each other. They don't have a grandma. It would be hard for her to get out fast. Fires are noisy. Firemen and policemen are yelling into their radios.

More trucks and cars with sirens and an ambulance scream up to the police tape. A bunch of kids give big cheers when there's a crash like the floor breaking through or glass breaking. I'll go around to the other side to get away from them.

Something's burning down the alley. Sparks must have landed there. Somebody's garage?

It's the shed! What about Cat? What about the kittens? Get out of my way, all of you, I've got to get there. I've got to help Cat.

• • •

"Cat, Cat, are you out? Come, Cat-Cat. Can you hear me?" She's still in there with the kittens. If I hurry I can get them out the window. I can't let them burn up. My board comes off easy.

There's already fire in here. It's so smoky. I pull my shirt over my mouth and nose. My dad would say, "Stupid Du, don't go in there." It's hot but there's not as much smoke if I crawl on the floor. My dad would be so mad if he knew I was doing this. My grandma would be worried for Cat too. She would help me. I'll shove the trash can upside down over the burning stuff. Maybe the fire won't spread.

Shoot! I can't see. My eyes hurt. The roof won't fall in, will it? I hope the roof won't fall in. Where is Cat? "Cat, Cat, are you here?" I gotta hurry. The floor is hot. I'm never gonna tell my dad I did this.

Somebody's outside yelling. That old man. It's his shed. He's yelling and rattling on the door. I know he can't open that lock in the dark. I wish he could. I could get out of here. He's not yelling at me. He's yelling, "Kitty, kitty, kitty." I wish he could open the door. I'll be stuck if anything falls. Where's Cat? The old man gave up. He's gone away. Kitten! Here, little kitten. I've got you.

"You get out of there, kid. Get out of there right now. Do you hear me?" The old man's back, yelling. He's yelling at me to get out but now I can reach the kittens. Cat's not here. There are only four kittens. "Cat, where are you?" Shoot! The trash can's burning. It smells awful. What if I can't get back to the window? The floor's too hot. Sticky, smelly plastic from the trash can on the floor. Can I get back? I'll just wrap the kittens in my shirt. "It's okay, kittens. Let me get ahold of you."

I'm scared. I don't know if I can get back to the window. It was stupid to come in here. It's too hot and I can't breathe.

Oof! Water! Water's spraying across the floor. Water, water, keep coming, keep coming. Let me just get to the window. I can see now from those flames near the roof hole. What if the roof falls? I don't care how hot the floor is. I'm getting out of here. Water, keep coming.

I stick my head out the window. Real air. It's so cold and good. I push my shirt-bag of kittens through. I'm going to get out. I don't want to land on the kittens. Let go with my feet. Fall to the ground. Ow! I'm down. I lost my shoe in there. I'm not dead. My dad's going to be mad about my shoe. Where's Cat?

I breathe deep, deep breaths of air. I'm glad I'm cold with no shirt. I'm wet all over, clothes and skin and hair and feet, one with a shoe and one without. The shirtful of kittens is dripping too. There's the old man. He's on his hands and knees in front of the shed door. His hose is stuck under the door. He's still spraying water in there and yelling.

"I'm out," I yell back. "I'm out." We stare at each other in the wild light from the flames. He struggles up from the ground.

"It's gonna fall," he shouts, waving his arms for me to get back. We both back away. A terrible loud crash and sparks shoot in all directions. The shed roof caves in. I'm shaking. What if I was still in there? I hug my wet shirtful of kittens.

The old man's face looks scary, lit by the sparks and

flames. He stares at his shed. "Is the cat in there?" He nods at my shirt.

"Kittens," I answer. We both look back at the flaming shed. Only four kittens. Cat must have rescued one. A fire truck with a siren and flashing lights comes roaring down the alley.

I push the wet shirtful of kittens into the old man's hands. I run and vault the fence at the back of my yard. "Stop! Come back!" yells the old man.

Bright flames light the alley. Just what I thought. Cat is lying by the break in the back of the shed. I pick her up. She doesn't move. There is no kitten. The wooden gate in the old man's back wall opens. I make it through with heavy Cat just before the fire engine roars to a stop. I push her into the old man's arms. I run back through the gate.

"Get outa here, kid!" the fireman roars at me above the sound of the truck engine and the rushing water and crackling flames. He's high on his truck. He can't get me. Fire truck lights blind me as I splash through the alley in front of the truck. Cat took her kitten across the alley behind the garbage-can fence. I'm sure of it. "Get outa here!" the fireman yells again.

I jump out of sight behind the cans. My hands feel around in the wet muck of the alley. Something is squishy. I grab it. I run behind the truck. I scramble over my back fence and the side fence back to the old man. He has limp Cat in one arm and the shirtful of kittens in the other. He pushes me hard toward his door with the bag of kittens. "Go, go," he shouts. Water from the hoses pours into the shed.

More sparks shoot up as the walls cave in. I walk backward, staring, as the firemen pour on more water. I was in there. The old man dumps Cat back in my arms. I hug her but she doesn't move. I hand him the soggy body of the kitten. "Come inside," he says.

I follow him into his house. It's warm there but I can't stop shaking. Water drips on his kitchen floor. He disappears down the hall. I lean down to Cat. I breathe on her nose. I whisper, "Cat, Cat, your kittens need you." The old man comes back with a load of stuff. Cat's slits of eyes open. "She's alive," I whisper.

He nods. "Sure she is," he says. He throws me a towel. He kneels on the floor to make a bed with a box and more towels. He empties the kittens out of my shirt into it. They mew and cry. All but the last one I found. It's wet and skinny and still. Cat twists out of my arms. I put her with them. She falls over but she licks them. She licks the still one roughly. It doesn't move. I kneel with the old man. We rub Cat and the kittens dry with the towels. He tosses me an old T-shirt. "Don't have any shoes," he says. I shrug.

The old man clears his throat. "You're very brave," he says in a louder voice, "very smart to get the cat from the alley. To find the kitten." I look at him. He's got the same mean look he has when he looks through our window. "You're also pretty darn foolish," he adds. He's not being mean. He's saying *brave* and *smart* about me. *Foolish* too but that doesn't matter. I shake again thinking of the smoke and the burning floor and the falling roof.

"I couldn't get out without the water," I say. He looks down and gently rubs one of the kittens.

"Do you feed her?" I ask.

"Yes," he answers. "Do you?"

I nod. "She's a smart cat," I say. We both rub the kittens. They make little noises as they find a place to nurse. They are so happy to be safe and warm with their mother.

The old man rubs the one from the alley. He rubs and rubs. "Yep," he whispers. I look at his face. I think he's smiling. The softest little squeaky sound from under the towel makes Cat lift her head. The face of the little still kitten pushes out of the folds. Another pitiful squeak. The kitten is alive. The old man gently moves the other kittens aside to make room. The little kitten drinks. Cat purrs.

I look out of his kitchen window. There is a light on in our house. I jump up. "I have to go home. I have to tell my grandma I'm okay."

"Yes," he says. "She'll be worried." For a moment we look directly at each other. I am thinking that she had good reason to worry and, a little bit, I feel the fear from the time in the shed. We both know what could have happened.

"Come see them tomorrow," the old man says. "On Christmas."

"Okay," I answer. I run home through the smoky air with one shoe. The trucks are still flashing at the end of the alley but the flames are gone.

When I run up the porch stairs, the door opens. My grandma is there, dressed, ready to go out. "I'm okay," I say quickly. "I'm sorry I made you worry. There's a fire. . . . That big old cat was in the shed with her kittens but I got them out . . . we got them out. The old man helped me."

She puts her hand on my arm. She feels that it's cold and I'm shaking. "Yes, Du, you're all right," she says, nodding. "You tell me about it in the morning." I'm still shaking when I lie down on the couch. She comes to make sure I'm covered. Usually I go in her room and pull up her covers.

Christmas Morning

The fire. I can smell it when I wake up. I lie on the couch and wonder when I can go to the old man's house and see Cat and her kittens. Today is Christmas but to me it's just Saturday. The only difference is nobody's around in the house. I check the kitchen but my grandma's still asleep. Tomorrow is Sunday. The day of the paper route. I'll get up at three, when it's still dark, to take all the papers. I wonder how many. I'm going to go outside now that it's light and see about the fire.

The only thing left of the shed is the door standing up

with no walls. It's still locked but the lock is too blackened now to see the numbers. Everything inside's all burned and wet. Here's my shoe. It feels funny on my foot. It kind of melted and it looks funny because it's darker than the other one. Anthony will laugh at how my shoes don't match. I hope my dad doesn't notice.

The handle burned off the lawn mower. Everything that's left is soggy wet. The trunk burned with the old man's picture book and his tree lights. The box with the building set burned too but the metal pieces are all scattered here on what's left of the trunk bottom. It's like soup with water and soggy paper and ashes but the pieces are okay. The little car I made still rolls. Everything stinks of smoke.

Trash cans are spilled all over the alley in the puddles. A lot of people are outside down by the burned apartments. I guess their presents burned up.

There's my grandma on the back porch. That means food. I take off my shoes by the door. She looks at the one that is smoky, dark and melted.

"A terrible fire for people, Du," she says. My grandma knows that whatever I did is already done. She won't tell me that I was stupid or foolish.

"The old man says I can come see the cat and her kittens," I tell her.

She doesn't say anything about Cat. "Does the old man have a name?" she asks. I don't answer but I know what she means. I eat a big bowl of hot noodles.

I mess around helping my grandma make the Christmas cake. It's a lot like the moon cake but with no egg yolks for moons. I break three eggs with one hand and stir with the other.

The old man comes outside to the shed. I want to see Cat. I go out like I'm looking for something in the yard. He sees me and nods. I help him save what's left of the lawn mower.

"I'll make a new handle," he says.

"I'll help," I say, and he doesn't say no. I would like to know how to do that.

He goes back where the shed mess is. I help him drag soggy sacks of grass seed and fertilizer to the trash. He scoops up what's left of the Christmas lights and throws them in. I wonder if he's ever going to go inside so I can see Cat.

He puts the burned-up picture book with the lawn mower. Maybe some of the pictures in the middle will be okay when it dries. He sees the pile I made of the pieces from the building set. He collects them all in a towel so I help him look for more of the pieces.

"You made some nice stuff," he says. I don't look at him. He knew all the time I was sneaking in there. "We'll go inside and get this stuff dried off." Finally. I carry the pieces of the metal set in the towel. He carries the picture book.

Cat is very happy in the box with her kittens. I think it's kind of funny that I thought the old man would hurt her when he was really feeding her just like I was. I feel a little sad because now my cat belongs to him. I kind of want him to know that I don't care that he won. At least I don't care very much. "I guess she found a place to live," I say. "She's your cat now."

He pets her for a minute. "I believe she's our cat," he says. "She'll live in my house and your yard." I think he smiles because we both know about my yard, how much Cat likes the weeds. "You can visit her here whenever you want," he adds.

She knows me. She lets me pet her and pick up the kittens. I offer her some fish I brought her wrapped up in a napkin in my pocket but it has paper stuck to it. She doesn't want it. The old man has bowls of food and water next to her box. A yellow kitten is crawling around in there away from Cat. I offer the fish to him. He licks it a little. He is the bravest one. I like him.

It's strange being in the old man's house. It has the same rooms as our house but it is so quiet, no radio, no TV, no talking. Everything is put away like no one lives here. Maybe that's why he looks through his window at our house all the time. I want to look through the old man's window where he sees into our dining room but I don't want to leave the kitchen unless he tells me to. I don't want him to get mad and not let me visit Cat. It's Christmas Day when Americans have turkeys and singing and presents and stockings full of toys but there's nothing here. His Christmas lights are in the trash. He doesn't have a tree anyway.

I pet the brave kitten. The old man is putting the pieces of the building set on the table. He's so slow. Like my grandma. One piece at a time. I would just dump them all out. He's rubbing each little piece with a rag and some oil. He's got my little car.

"Here," he says, holding it out to me. "You better take this car apart and dry it off. Then you can put it back together." This is just what I want to do. I sit at the table with him. He gives me a rag. He makes sure I use just a little bit of oil, which I already know.

"Nice," he says when I finish the car. "Did you ever make a windmill?" I shake my head because I'm not sure what a windmill is.

"Like this," he says, searching for a part.

"What's your name?" I blurt because I don't know if it's okay just to ask like that.

"Benjamin Wiezekowski," he says. Now I'm stuck. I can't remember it all even to say it now. I don't like it when people don't say my name right.

"Ben," he says. I'm still stuck. He is my friend now and to call him Ben like he was a kid at school sounds wrong to me. As bad as *old man*.

"Mr. W., if you like," he says. How does he know what I'm thinking?

"Okay, Mr. W., I'm Du," I say, which is all I can think of.

"How do you do, Du?" he says but I know he is not laughing at my name. I know from the book about the skinny girl in the covered wagon that this is how Americans said hello a long time ago.

"How do you do?" I say. We keep polishing. "Is that boy in the picture book your son?" I ask. Now he knows I'm a spy too. He keeps polishing but he looks up at me from under his bushy eyebrows.

"Yes." He nods. "He was quite a ballplayer. Couldn't get anywhere with it, though. He's in Alaska someplace now. It's too far to visit."

I don't ask any more. I know how my mom feels that her family is far away. I guess it happens to Americans too. I hope he can save some of his pictures from the middle of the book. I'm glad he doesn't say anything about how I gave away his oranges. I wish I didn't do that.

Cat is purring so loud it sounds like a motor. The kittens sleep next to her except for the brave yellow one, who bumps along the corners of the box. I laugh when he jumps clumsily on Cat's tail as she twitches it. The old man, Mr. W., looks up and laughs too. Cat doesn't mind. Through slitted eyes she watches us at the table. We don't talk much except when he tells me about the gears for the windmill. Cat sleeps.

"Okay, now you be the wind, Du," Mr. W. says, holding the windmill out to me. I blow. The blades whirl around faster and faster as I puff. I can see the gears working at the bottom.

"Someday I'll show my grandma the cat," I say softly.

"Bring her over today if you want," says Mr. W. I hoped he'd say that.

When I go to the door Cat jumps out of the box and follows me. I try to block her from getting out with my foot but she is quick like a shadow out the door. "It's okay," says Mr. W. "She'll come back."

Delicious cake smells meet me when I open the door. I tell my grandma that Mr. W. invited us to his house so she could see Cat. She takes a long time getting ready. Last, she covers the cake with a lace cloth from her room and puts on her hat. I carry the cake.

I look around for Cat while my grandma and I walk down our front walk, along the sidewalk, in his gate, around to the back of his house and up his back porch stairs. It's lots faster to jump over the fence, and the long walk gives me time to get worried. She doesn't speak English much and he doesn't speak Vietnamese. I don't want to talk for them. I won't know what to say. I wonder if we should go home. Before I can decide, Mr. W. opens the back door. Welcome, he bows. My grandma bows back. Cat streaks in the open door. She came from nowhere. We all laugh. We watch while she licks every kitten in the box. "Nice kitty," says Mr. W. as she settles among the kittens. How content they all are now, purring and pushing at her. Cat doesn't know my grandma but she is happy to let my grandma stroke her side.

Mr. W. has set his kitchen table with three places. He shows my grandma a can of something called oyster stew. "For Christmas lunch," he says.

She shows him the golden cake. She has made a little holly leaf design with green sugar icing around the top. "For Christmas lunch," she says. He understands her.

We eat the oyster stew, which is lots better than the canned noodle soup. We eat the cake, which is delicious. Mr. W. eats two pieces and so do I. The kittens are asleep so Mr. W. puts his bowl on the floor near the box. Cat jumps out to lick up the last of the oyster stew. I look quickly at my grandma but she is only smiling a little when the cat eats from a table dish. After dinner we show her the windmill and the car I made. I am happy that my grandma and Mr. W. are okay without too much talking. Maybe because they are both old. When we go home my grandma gives Mr. W. the rest of the cake.

"Merry Christmas, Mr. W.," she says, and then adds very slowly, "You very nice to Du."

"Merry Christmas, madam," says Mr. W. "He's a fine boy." We say good-bye to Cat and the kittens and go home.

Deadline

Vuong's alarm clock beeps loudly at three a.m. Last night I put it across the room so I'd have to get up to turn it off. I don't want to be late for the newspaper delivery. The night is dark and cold and quiet except for the beep. I jump up. I get dressed and run outside to wait.

It's cold so I jump up and down the stairs. In the Philippines one of the places we lived had a ladder instead of stairs. I climbed the ladder to get in but mostly I jumped out. I could jump and land on my feet and be running down the road before the other kid that lived there with his aunt had his feet on the ladder. If you jumped you didn't have to go down backward. I wonder if the other kid got to America. That ladder is like a dream memory now. I don't think about the Philippines much anymore. As my mom says, "You're here now."

I'm trying not to think about my dad and the paper route either because last night something else happened that he won't like. His boss, Mr. Vronsky, called. He wanted my dad to go fix someone's plumbing on Christmas. He was mad my dad wasn't home because that meant Mr. Vronsky had to do it himself. He yelled over the phone that my dad better call him the "minute he gets home or think about finding another job." I'm supposed to say this to my dad. He'll be mad at me if I do and mad at me if he doesn't get Mr. Vronsky's message. What if something gets messed up about the paper route too?

No one drives down the street in the middle of the night. The streetlight shows only our tall weedy grass and the sidewalk and the cars parked along the street. It's so quiet I can hear the freeway traffic blocks away. Maybe the papers won't come.

A white van screeches around the corner at the end of the block. I run out to the curb. "Where's your dad?" barks the driver.

"He'll be right out," I lie. I hope the guy doesn't wait. He leaves the van motor running and jumps out. Another guy opens the back. He starts tossing out bundles of papers. Heavy bundles bound with metal strips. One. Two. Three. Four. Five. They're still coming. The guy on the ground clips the metal strips and the top papers slide off onto our front walk. "You know how to do these?" the driver asks. I don't know what to say. Maybe I'm supposed to know. "Where's your dad?"

"I'll tell him," I say. He takes the top paper from one of the piles, folds it up, stuffs it into a plastic bag. "Every one of these gotta be out by seven at the latest," he warns. "Here's the route." He shoves a bunch of papers into my hand. "Tell your dad they gotta be near the door." A speaker squawks from inside the van. The driver and the other guy climb in quickly and drive away. Papers block our walk. I sit on one bundle to look at the route sheet. I don't even know where most of the streets are. My dad is going to be so mad. Thuy and Lin and Vuong are going to say how stupid I am. But they can't say I'm stupid if I do it.

My hands are so cold they won't fold as fast as I want them to. Plastic bags won't open right. They slip off the piles I make. To warm up I run down the street with ten papers. At least I know the houses on our street. I get the papers near the door. My melted shoe is still a little damp.

I come back. The pile of papers looks just as big as before. A light goes on in Mr. W.'s kitchen. His front door opens. He shuffles down the porch and across the lawn. I don't want him to know I am doing something foolish again. He will tell me it can't be done, to deliver all these papers by seven. I don't look up.

"Quite a job," he says.

"I guess," I say. He doesn't say anything else. He starts folding papers with me but he's slower than I am. He picks

193

up the route sheets. "I'll go fix this," he says. "Get me out of the cold." He takes the route sheets with him into his house. I'm not ready for them anyway. I fold and fold and fold. I think I'll run out of plastic bags but there are just enough. I need the route sheets.

"Here you go," he says. I didn't even see him come out, I was so busy folding. He hands me the sheets. He has drawn a map of the streets on a piece of paper on top. He has circles and squares and squiggles around the different houses that are near each other. On the map I see that some houses are across the freeway. He hands me a big shopping bag. I load it with papers. I run off to the next block. The sky is not so dark. I will never deliver all the papers by seven. I run faster as the bag gets lighter.

Now there are cars on the street and a few people out. It's still dark. Two more papers in this bunch. At the corner I see a kid out already in a red jacket on a skateboard. "Hi, Dude," he yells happily. It's Todd. "I got a skateboard for Christmas. I'm trying it out."

I wave. "I'm delivering papers," I yell. "I gotta finish by seven." He skateboards along behind me.

I run home for papers. From down the block I can see Mr. W. bending over the piles of papers. He's stuffing them all in grocery bags with the route sheets on each bag. "Deliver to the houses across the freeway," he says. "That's the hardest." I get a bag in each hand. Todd grabs one. He leaves his skateboard on my porch. We run slowly and breathe hard because the bags are heavy. They bounce around in their slippery plastic bags. We're both panting and slowing down with three blocks more to the freeway bridge.

A truck pulls up next to us. "Hey, what's happening?" It's the Mexican guy who fixes trucks down our block.

"Delivering papers," I yell.

"Jump in. I'll drop you off." He opens the door of the truck. Todd and I heave the newspapers on the floor of the cab. We climb in. I show the guy the map. We are across the freeway in a few minutes.

"Thanks a lot," Todd says when we jump out. I remember that is what Americans say all the time. I remember the clock on the dashboard too. Twenty minutes after six. We can never finish in time. My dad will lose the job. Still I run. Todd is running with me. He is having fun but I feel like the first day of American school when I knew nothing would work out right. Try as hard as you can but it will not be right. Why the heck did I say I'd do this?

We deliver all the papers across the freeway. We are good now at throwing them near the door. My arm aches. We run for home and more papers. It's too late. The clock at the 7-Eleven says 7:05.

I'm looking at my feet as I run. My foot hurts in the burned shoe. Maybe nobody'll notice if the papers are a little late. We run down the middle of the street. We run between the parked cars. We run panting to my house. I stop so fast Todd bumps into me.

The papers are all gone. The bags are all gone. Somebody

stole them. Todd runs up the steps to check his skateboard. I sink down on the steps. I will have to tell my dad.

Mr. W. is gone. No light comes from his windows. He should have stayed to protect the papers. A second later I know this isn't fair. Mr. W. helped me in the middle of the night. He didn't have to help at all. It's my own fault. Todd sits down next to me.

"Nobody wants to steal a bunch of newspapers," he says. True. They read it once. They throw it in the trash. Maybe the delivery guys came and took their papers back. Cars pass along our street now.

I am tired and hungry and my arm aches and my foot hurts in the melted shoe but I don't care about any of that. I'm sad because I couldn't deliver the newspapers. I'm sad even if my dad never finds out. I almost did it. If they were here I would deliver them all just a little late. But they aren't. I don't even care that Todd sees that I'm sad. He sits next to me spinning the wheels of his skateboard. Not saying anything.

"Du!" I look up. My dad's car is in the street next to the parked cars. He's yelling at me.

"Here we go," I whisper to myself. I drag over to the car. My dad rolls down the window. I look at him. I am face to face looking at him like an American kid. He is grinning. This must be the way he looks when he wins the pot gambling with my uncles during Tet.

"Hey! Way to go!" he says, also like an American. Then he switches to Vietnamese. "We did it," he says, grinning.

"It's seven o'clock and they're all delivered." I can't believe it for a minute. Why is he here? How does he know about the delivery time? He laughs at my confusion.

"Who do you think saved you by delivering the rest of those papers?" he asks proudly. I know it was him.

"How did you know?" I ask.

"Grandma called me at four-fifteen. She said you were doing the paper route and it was a big job. I drove home in less than two hours. No traffic."

"When I got here I saw those bags of papers stacked all over the sidewalk with the man next door here watching them. He showed me the delivery route maps he made. I delivered all of them." He laughs. "You were gonna run your shoes off getting yourself in trouble, lazy boy." He is proud of the work I did, of how hard I tried. "Grandma always said you were just like me when I was young in Vietnam. At first I didn't believe her." He's not laughing anymore. "Now I see. You do it your own way. Like me. That neighbor says you were brave in the fire and helped him. He thinks you're quite a kid."

"How come I'm like you in Vietnam?" This is what I want to hear. How can my grandma say this? How can it be true? I thought my dad and me were as different as birds are from fish . . . or water buffalo from reindeer.

He's laughing again. "You're up at three in the morning."

"Did you deliver papers?" I ask.

"No," he laughs. "I got up to go fishing."

"Fishing is more fun," I say.

"And you're a little crazy. You think you can do anything, like me," he answers, but he laughs again and looks proud. "Together we did the job."

A car honks. It is stuck behind him in the narrow street. "Don't wake Grandma," he says. He hands me a couple of dollars. "You and your friend get some donuts." He doesn't give away money but he believes in paying for work done. The car honks again. "I'll go back to Orange to get the others." As he pulls away he shouts back, "Du, you and me have a paper route."

Todd lets me ride his skateboard partway to the donut shop. I'm not bad at it but I'm going to get better. I can make a board if I can find some wheels. The donut shop is warm. It smells wonderful. We get a box of donuts. We eat them as we walk down the street. We'll go see if Gil and Martin are around. We save two donuts for them. I'll take them all to see Cat later. Mr. W. won't mind. I'll thank him for his help like an American kid.

● ● ●

In the afternoon I go home so I'll be there when they come from Orange. I forgot to tell my dad about Mr. Vronsky calling too. Thuy and Lin and Vuong come up the front walk like they're so tired they can hardly stand up. I jump off the porch to check out their bags. Even though we don't do Christmas they have some presents, sweaters for all of them, and Thuy and Lin have some earrings. My mom gives me a bag from my uncle with a football in it. I'm going to trade it for a soccer ball. Everyone asks me about the fire. I tell them about the apartment building and the people outside and the trucks and the flames. "I had to get that cat and her kittens out of the shed" is how I end.

Vuong looks at my wrecked shoe. "You're crazy, Du," he says. "Just like that bearded guy said."

I remember how my dad was so mad when the bearded dad told him what I'd done to get the free chickens and hitting Andy's sister. Vuong can read my face. "I told him how it really happened on the way to Orange," Vuong says. "Lin told him about that math contest you won. You have to find a good time to tell him stuff."

"Is it a good time now?" I ask. "Because I've got something to tell him."

Vuong laughs but I'm not laughing. "Try him and see," says Vuong. I go help my dad take bags and boxes of stuff out of the trunk.

I decide the best way is to just say it right out. "Mr. Vronsky called," I say. "He wants you to call him the minute you get home because he has a job." I wait. I don't look at his face but I see his hand tighten and the jerk he gives the box he's lifting.

"You know what we're going to do with our paper route money?" he asks. I shake my head. "We're going to put it in the savings account I started for a van. It's going to be my own plumbing van and I'm going to say good-bye very soon to Mr. Vronsky. And when it's not a plumbing van there'll be plenty of room in it for everybody to go to Orange with us."

I'm glad we'll all be able to go to Orange together but I'm happiest my dad won't have to work for Mr. Vronsky anymore. I'm happiest that I'm the one helping him get the van.

"After that we'll buy a bike," he adds. I shrug but I hear him. We take the bags and boxes inside. It's a good day. Everything turned out okay and I've got a lot of stuff to do.

About the Author

Linda Himelblau taught for thirteen years in a San Diego school where twenty-three languages were spoken by students from all over the world. She admired the skills, stories, and games they brought with them, especially fast-paced marble games and rubber-band jump rope. She helped some of her students learn soccer and coached a team for five years. She lived in San Diego with her husband, Irv, and their cat, Daisy. Linda Himelblau died in early 2005.